THE
PROSPER CHRONICLES

BOB WOOD

MEZCALITA
PRESS

MEZCALITA PRESS, LLC
Norman, Oklahoma

FIRST EDITION
Copyright © 2018 by Robert E. Wood
All Rights Reserved
ISBN-13: 978-0-9994784-2-4

Library of Congress Control Number: 2018952025

No part of this book may be performed, recorded, thieved, or otherwise transmitted without the written consent of the author and the permission of the publisher. However, portions of poems may be cited for book reviews—favorable or otherwise—without obtaining consent.

Cover Design: Jen Rickard Blair
Cover Photo: Derek Klingenberg

MEZCALITA PRESS, LLC
Norman, Oklahoma

The Prosper Chronicles

Bob Wood

Table of Contents

Preacher's Kid … … 3
Belt Buckle … … 8
Just Burnt Beans and Hot Water … … 12
Reunion … … 19
Dry Creek Anthology … … 25
Reinforcement … … 30
Bingo … … 34
Mary's Free Will Café … … 39
Tumbleweeds … … 44
Maydean … … 52
Zero … … 60
Froggy McNamara … … 66
Lovey … … 72
Charlotte's Interweb … … 80
MacGregors of Broken Toe Ranch … … 85
BJ's Dog, Charlie … … 93
Rumor Mill … … 99
Nature or Nurture … … 104
Coach Tom's Laundry … … 110
Nighthorse Roundup … … 116
Frank Bonner, in Memoriam … … 124
Archie … … 128
Chauncey Cooter … … 139
Changin' Your Plaque … … 148
Eden … … 157
Ruby Foster … … 165

Acknowledgements

The fictional town of Prosper chronicled herein should not be confused in any way, shape or form with the actual town of Prosper, Texas. The name was just too perfect so I borrowed it shamelessly for the nefarious purpose of this collection.

Don't ask me who's influenced me. A lion is made up of the lambs he's digested, and I've been reading all my life.

~ Giorgos Seferis, writer, diplomat, Nobel laureate (1900-1971)

Many poets and other writers whom I have tasted have inspired me to read poetry and to write. Traces of many of them can be found herein: David Lee, Garrison Keillor, Harry Chapin, Anne Lamott, Billy Collins, William Stafford, Stephen Crane, Ted Kooser, Nathan Brown, Beth Wood... I extend my gratitude to all of them.

Thanks to my father, Robert E. Wood, Sr. who instilled in me an awe of the power of poetry.

Thanks to the Lubbock Buds. You encouraged me when I didn't deserve it and laughed at the right places.

Thanks and a tip of the cowboy hat to Derek Klingenberg of Klingenberg Farms Studios for the cover photo which definitely has overtones of Broken Toe Ranch.

Thanks to Nathan, Ashley, and Jen for your support and expert assistance. You literally made this possible.

And special thanks to Ann Wood, my wife, lover, best friend, life companion and encourager-in-chief.

"Life in Lubbock, Texas taught me two things: One is that God loves you and you're going to burn in hell. The other is that sex is the most awful, filthy thing on earth and you should save it for someone you love."

~ **Butch Hancock,
singer-songwriter (1945-)**

The Prosper Chronicles

Preacher's Kid

Town o' Prosper was seriously overnamed.
Never had more than one traffic light
and that was just a blinkin' yellow.
Had a bank once't but it went belly up
lendin' money to farmers for their crops.

Shoot, every farmer in the county
has gone busted at least once't
what with drought and hail
and weather actin' generally weird.
Always too much rain, too little
or at just the wrong time
too cold, too hot or crop prices gone all
whomper-jawed — there's a thousand ways
to go busted as a farmer.
New banker shoulda known better.

Heck, he even lived here once't before.
Family wasn't farmers though.
Papa was a preacher at the Methodist Church
the one on Main Street usta be kinda leanin'
so's only the bell tower was standin' straight.
He went off to college — left Prosper behind.
Most of the kids who get away
never circle back — cain't says I blame 'em.

Anyway this preacher's kid banker
come back and bought the bank.

Idea come to him when he was packin' up
his momma's house after she passed.
Hadn't been back to Prosper
but four or five times in forty years
two of 'em was for funerals.

But right off he stepped in too deep
even loanin' money to BJ the town drunk
or at least one of the leading candidates.
BJ couldn't make a crop if the good Lord
installed a sprinkler system for him.

The onliest year I can recollect when
the cotton was good and the prices stayed up
('cause the Chinese or somebody
had just discovered blue jeans).
BJ managed to miss out
on accounta being late defoliatin'.
Was wiped out by a hellacious storm
that come up outta nowhere.
Hail knocked that cotton plumb to the ground
— covered his field from turnrow to turnrow
with a speckled blanket of stalks stickin' up
all the bolls and fibers mashed to the ground.
Nothing left a picker could pick
or even a Mexican.

BJ got the great idea that he might could just
roll up that speckled blanket.

Tried to harvest it with a front end loader
but the gin said they couldn't take it
— might gum up the works.
Said they might when he first brung it up
but then didn't — cain't says I blame 'em.
It was a mess, but a mess that coulda been
a helluva resurrection story if it'd worked.
Crop insurance folks was sure pullin' for him.
'Course he didn't have none but others did.
Still a pretty good idea for a lazy drunk
but I guess not so smart after all.

So when preacher's kid bought the bank
was the onliest year didn't nobody need a loan
to get their seed and fertilizer and diesel.
He just spent his time that year
howdyin' folks around town
and all over Shoemaker County
sponsorin' watermelon picnics
and little league teams and joinin'
the onliest Bible study group at First Presby
even though he was a life-long Methodist.
Heck he already knew all the Methodists.

Told me straight up he was class of '59 PHS.
Onliest class I can recollect
never won a single football game.
Played six-man like they do now
and scores could really get up there

but they lost them all
most by the mercy rule.

Class of '59 had Joe Bob Frasher too
most famous person ever out of Prosper.
Got in with a political crowd in college
and got hisself elected a state senator
and then got hisself convicted of a few
million in kickbacks on state contracts.
Joe Bob and Prosper was on the big-time
New York City CBS News
when he hired a guy to kill the judge
and the guy was a cop and didn't do it.
Fella drove down all the way from
New York City to stand in front of the house
Joe Bob growed up in and tell the world
about a guy from Prosper.

Anyhow, after he bought the bank
preacher's kid saw more and more farmers
quittin' farming — selling to big corporations
who didn't borrow from the Bank of Prosper
and didn't keep any deposits there either.
And when they sold, most of the farmers
joined their kids in big cities or on the coast
out of the dust and the wind
and away from the ghost of Prosper
taking their rainy day funds with them.
Those who did stay and who farmed

and borrowed from the bank
hit a long streak of spindly-sticked crops.
Couldn't repay the loans.
Asked for more to plant bigger the next year.
Onliest way to get back to even
was to have a good year with high prices
but weather and prices said *no* to the farmers
and *no* to the Bank of Prosper.

By then the preacher's kid
was hell-bent to stay in Prosper
even after the bank bellied up.
Heck folks don't blame him for the shutdown.
He was mostly just tryin' to help neighbors.
So at the Wednesday Forty-Two game
down at Jerry Don's John Deere
someone ast him what he was gonna do.
I've already got it figured out he said.
I'm fixin' to buy the cemetery and funeral home.
Folks has all gotta die eventually.

Guess he never noticed that folks was leavin'
Prosper before they left these earthly bonds.
But come to think of it I never heard of
a cemetery going busted
and if he's the last one standing in Prosper
reckon he'll just have to bury hisownself.

BELT BUCKLE

When the preacher's kid come back
to Prosper and bought the bank
some people didn't even know who he was.

Preacher hisself had been gone
nigh unto twenty years.
Went to sleep drivin' home
from a late night revival.
Stuck it in the bar ditch.
Mighta walked away
but the car hit the culvert
on the Simpson's pasture road.
Stopped the car pretty solid.
He ended up in the back seat.

Those who remember the funeral
remember the boy.
He came back, stood with his momma
stayed a coupla days then went back to
wherever it was he was from then.
He had to come back a couple years later
to stand for his momma.
Two funerals in two years was a bit much.

When word got around Prosper
that Robert Alvis Taylor had bought the bank
some people said *Who the hell is that*
and some said *Hell that's Bobby Taylor*

the preacher's kid.
Me, I knew exactly who it was
but still wondered 'bout that **Alvis** deal.
Thought at first that it might be
just that momma couldn't spell
and was one o' them screamers who swooned
over that Presley kid but shoot
preacher's kid musta been born
way before all the fuss over Elvis
and sideburns and rock and roll.
What really struck me about the **Alvis** part
was how it really ruint his chances to wear
a belt buckle made with his initials.
Sometimes folks don't do much thinkin' over
namin' their kids —'specially preachers
but at least he wasn't Ezekiel or
Deuteronomy or somethin' like that.

Anyways, after he bought the bank
as he was acquaintin' hisself with all his
customers everyone called him Mr. Taylor
even folks older'n his dead parents.
When he said *Just call me Robert,* you coulda
knocked me over with a feather.
Never heard nothin' but Bobby before
when he was living here in Prosper.
Musta picked that Robert stuff up wherever
he's been being up 'til he come back.

Didn't matter anyhow.
Me and the boys at the Wednesday
Forty-Two game down at Jerry Don's
John Deere always just called him PK.
Not to his face and not when
we was doing any banking.
Wives did too 'til BJ the town drunk
slipped and said it to his face once't
and when he looked confused told him
'at was what everyone called him.
So he ast us at Forty-Two and we couldn't lie.
He just sat there thinkin' after we told him
— with that thousand-yard stare.

Then there was that mess-up
right after he bought the bank.
Sadie Allen was acrost the street from
the bank in Dub Lake's offices
fixin' to haggle over her auto insurance
and lookin' out the window.
She saw the new banker leavin' the bank
— musta looked startled 'cause Dub ast
What is it? Sadie says *It's Robert the banker.*
Now Dub's hearing ain't what it use't to be
or for that matter what it should be
and Sadie can be a little whispery and Dub
thought she said *Someone's robbin' the bank*
so he grabbed his phone and called Mary's
'cause Dub had just left there

and trooper Blackwell was there
sippin' coffee and eatin' donuts.
Tell trooper Blackwell that they's robbin' the bank
Dub said when Mary answered.
Mary did and trooper Blackwell seein' a man
he didn't know exitin' the bank
went into full hands-up mode.
Took a while to get things straightened out.
When trooper Blackwell brung Robert inside
to ast how much he got
Mozelle, the head teller that Robert
had good sense enough to keep
'cause she really ran the bank, said
There's been no robbery. That's our new banker.
Most of Shoemaker County got a good laugh
outta that when it got around
but not the new banker.
He'd thought he was gonna get shot right in front
of his veryown bank — by a certified law man.

Next Wednesday at the Forty-Two game
down at Jerry Don's John Deere
he just looked up and said
OK boys, PK it is. Just call me PK.
He almost cried a coupla weeks later
when me 'n the boys gave him
a big belt buckle with PK on it.

Just Burnt Beans and Hot Water

PK was running late this morning
so Mary was about to pour my second cup
when he walked through the door
went over and picked up his mug
sidled over sat down nodded to Mary
and said *Pour me one right from that pot.*

Mary and me looked at each other
'cause if PK was fixin' to drink a cup
of Mary's black as coal tar coffee
I was fixin' to win a bet.

When PK moved back to Prosper
and bought the bank he took up a habit
of coming in to Mary's every morning
nursin' a cup of coffee
while he planned his day.
Good way to visit with folks
and find out what was happening.

Shoot, I had been doing that
(except for the plannin' part)
since way before Mary changed the name
from Gross Café to Mary's Free Will Café.
I reckon I was Mary's regularest customer
and Mary and I had a regular long-running
palaver that pretty much covered everything
from the trick play in Friday's football game

to whether the universe is expandin' or
contractin' to where the hell was
global warming during the blizzard of '16.

Now I knowed who PK was even before
I saw him sitting drinking coffee and
I knowed that he just bought the bank
so I moseyed over and howdied him
and then left him to his plannin'.

Well I watched him pretty carefully from
acrost the room without really lookin' at him
and I seen him the first day reach
in his pocket, pull out a small silver flask
and pour something in his cup
which was full of Mary's coffee
that he had already ruint by putting
milk in it until it was the color
of Chauncey Cooter's buckskin nighthorse.

Over the weeks and months that followed
he wasn't nearly so secretive.
Weren't long the flask was on the table
along with a small snuff box that
he dipped into and sprinkled
the contents into his coffee.
He even got Mary to brew him a special pot
with coffee you could actually see through.
After a few more months he seemed to be

doin' a lot less plannin'
and a lot more lookin' around.
One morning he looked over and saw
me and Mary discussin' the topic of the day
which happened to be whether the stripes
in the Walmart parking lot
was commandment or merely suggestion.
He come over with all his paraphernalia
sat down and joined right in.
(He was for commandment.)

After that seems like his plannin' tapered off.
Him and me would meet might near
every morning for coffee
and whether or not Mary joined us
we solved or at least worked on
almost all the world's problems that
we could think of and some that
popped up unexpectedly.

One day I ast him *Robert*
('cause he hadn't yet cottoned to PK)
Robert I says *what exactly is it
you are puttin' in your coffee
and how come your'ra puttin' it there?*
Well he said pointing to the flask *this is caramel
and this* pointing to the snuff box
*is cinnamon cardamom and brown sugar.
You should try it* he says to me

handin' me the flask and shovin'
the snuff box across the booth.
No thanks I says *I like mine black*
— pure taste of the bean.
Been drinking it that way since I was three.
Always drink it black
never dilute it with milk or other contaminants.
Some day when I am feelin' braver
or closer to the edge I'll try a sip
doctored like yours 'cause I gotta put it
somewhere on the scale though I think I know
about where it will fall.

What scale? ast PK.
Well I says *being kinda an expert I've ranked all the*
coffee I've ever drank — created a scale so I can have
a simple and useable way to describe my coffee.

Number one is cowboy coffee.
Some folks say I should divide this up
between branding fire coffee and campfire coffee.
I see the point but today some branding irons
are electric or even chilled for freeze-branding
so the branding fire is just a campfire.
Anyway that's the top — but watch for the grounds.

Number two is Mary's coffee.
Mary looked up nodded and smiled.
Then truckstop coffee, made-at-home coffee

see-through coffee (I paused for emphasis)
then instant coffee, looks-like coffee
and anything below that is swill.
So it's an eight point scale
and I try to drink nothing below three.

Wow said PK *what about espresso*
and cappuccino?
What about French press, cold-brewed
where do they fit? What about Kopi Luwak?
That's supposed to be the best.

Don't know none of those, I says
and as long as I can get one through three
I am officially not interested.

PK later told me that he never drank coffee
at all until he was plumb growed up
and workin' in California.
Him and his friends would meet at Starburst's
and he tried everything he just named except
Kopi Luwak.

Suckered me right in so I ast
What's Kopi Luwak?
They don't sell it at Starburst's says PK
Supposed to be the best coffee
and the most expensive in the world.
Then he proceeded to tell me

that this civet cat in Asia
(kinda like a skunk) eats coffee beans
and craps them out — they are gathered
(how'd you like that job?)
roasted and made into coffee.
Sorry I don't care if it's the
least expensive coffee in the world
you couldn't pay me to drink that.
It automatically goes below swill.

Over the years drinkin' coffee together
'most every morning and sharin' opinions
and theories and even feelings
about all manner of things
me and PK became great friends.
I pretty much know what he thinks
about anything — he does me too.
He can finish my sentences and so can I, his.

Over the years I shamed him into
abandoning the caramel sauce.
I filched his snuff box once
when he wasn't lookin'
so he turned to sugar for his coffee.
I talked Mary into gradually thickenin'
his special pot of coffee to where
you couldn't see through it anymore.
And I sensed that when I took him
to a roundup with a branding fire

on a brisk October morning
with not one grain of sugar to be seen
there might be a breakthrough.

So here we were the next morning in Mary's.
Like I said PK comes in late
Mary pours him black coffee
from the regular pot per his request
then she went to servin' other customers.
I saw her keeping watch on us out of the
corner of her eye to see if
he loaded it up with sugar
and we both watched as PK raised
that mug to his lips and commenced to drink
hot and black straight out of the pot.

I felt like I had broken a range-wild colt.
Slowly but steadily PK had learned
how to drink a real cup of real coffee.

And a few minutes later I had
to explain it all to PK when Mary brought me
a piece of her pecan pie fixed just the way
I like it — covered in whipped cream
drizzled with caramel and chocolate.
Sorry she says *it's grande not venti.*

Reunion

Me and PK, the undertaker
was rehashin' Wednesday's Forty-Two game.
PK bought the cemetery and funeral home
after he run the bank into the ground
makin' bigger and bigger loans
to his neighbors who's tryin' to make a crop
in this God-forsaken land.

PK ain't never undertaken anybody
he's just the owner of the funeral home
and the cemetery and the official greeter.
It's Jeb Satterwhite that does the undertaking.
He's the one that went to mortuary school
but he's better with the dead ones
than with the mourners.
So he and PK make a pretty good team
'cause PK don't really like the dead ones
'cept as inventory for Beloved Rest Cemetery.

Anyhow me and PK was talkin'
some serious dominoes and
outta the clear blue sky he ups and says
I think I'm gonna organize
a 50th reunion for the class of '59.
Well I didn't want to piss in his campfire
but there ain't been no class reunion
in Prosper in whenever
far as my memory says.

No one who leaves
ever wants to reunite
and no one who stays
wants to see them who moved on.

How many was in your class? I ast him.
Nine walked across the stage he allowed
and Anna Hobbs got her diploma
from Mr. Cooper in his office
'cause she was married and
couldn't go to class or cross the stage with us.

Far as I could tell her and PK
was the onliest ones
still in Prosper from the class of '59.
How you gonna find the rest of them? I ast.
Said he'd use the interweb and some kinda
search engine — *Good luck* I says.
PK can hardly drive a stick-shift pickup.
Don't know how he figgered
he could drive a search engine.

About two weeks later PK crowed
Found Billy Ray Robinson and Hank Carter
both in Dallas — neither wants to come.
They both said the same thing: Are you kidding?
Johnny Mahan didn't make it out of Viet Nam.
Can be found now in Arlington, Virginia.
Got all the guys now except Hector Martinez

and he was hardly part of the class.
Moved here 'bout the same time I did,
in our senior year and left the next.
Don't expect he'd come back even if we found him.
Girls will be harder 'cause they marry
and change their names.

Only surviving parent of anyone
in the class of '59 livin' in or near Prosper was
Mrs. Hunt — Terry Mike's mom.
Next bit of sleuthin' PK done was to visit her
in the Happy Trails Living Center.
Ol' Mrs. Hunt didn't always remember
she had a daughter and she wasn't downright
sure of PK's motives in lookin' for her.
So after sittin' down to tea with PK
she excused herself and
went back to her room and went to sleep.
Waste of gas, that trip.

So let's do a tally I says to PK
Of six boys, you got
two in Dallas who won't come
Martinez — domicile unknown
Joe Bob Frasher still locked up in the big house
Johnny Mahan can't make it
and yourself.
Of the four girls you got
Anna Hobbs right here in Prosper

she ain't comin' to no reunion
Mary Mike Johnson
dead and permanently buried in Beloved Rest.
You got Terry Mike Hunt
best lookin' girl in the class
whose mom is loony and whose
whereabouts is also unknown.
Who does that leave?

Only Michelle LeMaster
says PK, kinda mopey
and I'm drawin' blanks in findin' her.
Guess I'll have to wait
for Joe Bob's parole to come up
before we can have a reunion.

What PK didn't know was that
I knowed a thing or two about the class of '59
and I been doin' my own sleuthin'.
Anna told me PK and Michelle
had been kinda sweet on each other
not serious sweet — Michelle was Catholic
— but kinda smile-across-the-room
sweet on each other.

And Anna thought Michele's sister was
a teacher in Sweetwater, last name Smith.
So I runs my traps
and gets in touch with Mrs. Smith.

She puts me on to Michelle.
I runs her down and find out
she's a new widow.
Husband died in a fire started by their cat.
She had went to college
had been on the rodeo team
moved to Austin
married a guy who sold computers
out of his dorm room
had five kids including a daughter
who was Miss October in Playboy magazine
sailed around the world with her husband
in their own considerable-sized boat
and even though she hadn't kept up
with no one in Prosper she would love
to come back to the reunion.

She ast me if PK was Bobby Taylor's
cousin or somethin' 'cause she knowed
Bobby was an only kid.
So's I told her that PK was him
and how PK got his name
and about the belt buckle and all
and she laughed and said she thought
that was pretty funny.

Later when PK was mopin' around about
the prospects of a reunion and tryin' to figure
if he could reunite with hisownself

I broke it to him about Michelle.
You'd a thought I'd clobbered him
with a sucker rod.

Anyway him and Michelle met on the phone
and planned and planned
and she come for homecoming
and he give her a great big mum
and they rode in the parade
on their very own 50th Reunion float
that was nothing more than a cotton trailer
with a little crepe paper
woven through the chicken wire.

I ast him how it went
Fine he says *She was nice*
but we're really different.
You're the one who found her he says
How come you didn't tell me?
Tell the truth
I knowed she was still Catholic
but I swear on the good book
I didn't know she was a Democrat.

Dry Creek Anthology

Shortly after PK come to Prosper
and bought Beloved Rest Cemetery
I offered to take him on a stroll
to acquaint him with the various sections
and markers inside its boundaries.

The southeast corner is the oldest
part of the cemetery.
Most of the markers there have
only names and dates
— early pioneers and settlers
who stretched the frontiers of civilization
sometimes farther than safety allowed.
Here is where you find

>   **Jonathan Grosbeck**
>   **1809-1854**

Original Grosbeck spread is now
called Chapparal Ranch
and the Murchison family who live there
are direct descendants
of old Jonathan himself.
Rock outcropping on the cliff face
of Bird Creek Canyon resembled the profile
of a man and was called Papa Jon
in honor of old Jonathan
until a couple of years ago

it crumbled and fell away after a summer rain.
Now it looks more like a local Indian chief
Rear-End-of-a-Wolf.
Still I keep on looking for Papa Jon
and he keeps on not bein' there.

Funniest part of the cemetery is
the southwest corner where
April Showers (1920-1949) is resting next to
Mae Flowers (1918-1973).
It's also where Ben Back is buried next to
Orville Flippen even though
Ben shot Orville on account of a bit of a
misunderstanding over a corncob pipe.
It has always been known as
the Back-Flippen shootout.

Down by the big oak tree is the final
resting place of Mary Ann Galway.
On the top of her stone is a brass oboe
The stone says

> Mary Ann Polk Galway
> 1936-2000
> Oboist
> FLOPO
> Best A in all the land

FLOPO stands for the Federated League

of Professional Oboists
an international musician's union.
Mary Ann was president from 1980-1986.
Mrs. Galway was a music teacher in Prosper
from the early 60's until the late 90's.
She was not just an oboist she was a
world-class world-famous oboist.
She taught so many kids from Prosper to play
the oboe that there were more oboes
than trombones in the marching band.
First chair oboist was the most prestigious
position in the high school
better than homecoming queen or
valedictorian — even better than quarterback.
It ain't never had an All-State football player
but Prosper has had an All-State oboist
almost every year for thirty years.
Kids knew that they could use the oboe
to escape Prosper.
It was the basis for many college scholarships
and a tuning resource for symphonies
all over the country and even the world.
One student, Jonas Nash, gained his
fifteen minutes of fame as oboist
in a punk rock band Bat Dung Fever.
Time magazine did a piece on Mrs. Galway
and her legendary impact on the world of oboes
naming her one of the one hundred
most influential musicians of the 1980's.

*Is that why Mary wears an oboe pin on her collar
ast PK, to honor Mrs. Galway?*
Not really I said
*That pin means Mary was first chair oboe
when she was in school.
Look around and you'll see others
Dub Lake, Mozelle Tinker, Scooter Rogers
even Buster Kaplan
especially on November 17
International Oboe Day* (started by FLOPO).
*In a case of Jeffersonian irony Mrs. Galway
died on November 17, 2000.
Guinness says that her funeral set a record
for the most oboes playing simultaneously.
I remember flocks of cranes circlin' overhead
confused and bewildered.*

Next we moseyed down to the back fence row.
Three markers there had all the proper
names and information
but on the back of the markers.
On the front, one simply had a six
one a four and one a three.
All the Prosper sports fans knew
it was the double play combination
from the 1948 Prosper State Champion
baseball team — Bivins to Carter to Hart
— six to four to three.

Following our tour me and PK
adjourned to Mary's for coffee.
After catching up on local news and a lively
discussion with Mary about whether El Niño
is the cause of polar ice cap melt or the result
PK says to me *Thanks for the tour but one thing
has been botherin' me and I can't figure it out.
Over in the Methodist section
right by where Mom and Dad rest
is a stone marked "Atheist."
I know for a fact that Sean McDonald
was a Methodist preacher.
How could he be an atheist?*

Well I says *it's both a cosmic joke
and a mean trick.
Seems that Brother Sean
considered himself a Theist
and requested it on his stone.
The monument people made a terrible assumption
and rather than **A Theist**
they simply put **Atheist.**
When it was brought to the attention of Sean's son
his only living heir he supposedly just smiled
and said It's OK, just leave it.*

PK being a preacher's kid hisownself
just smiled and said *OK I understand.*

Reinforcement

One day we's fishin' and I ast PK
where he got all his money.
I mean he come back to Prosper and
bought the bank and run it into the ground
and then he bought the funeral home and
cemetery and they ain't enough people
in the county dyin' as a regular thing
to keep that operation afloat.

That's why PK come up with the brilliant idea
of rentin' the hearse to fraternity boys
at the college down the road on days
when there weren't no funerals.
They had parties or secret meetings in it
or just used it as a bus to get everybody
around to their parties or secret meetings.

PK didn't even have to deliver the hearse
and the frat boys had to keep it full of gas.
He just took one of them frat boy's Corvette
as collateral and wouldn't give it back
'til he got the hearse and got paid.
Learned that collateral stuff
when he was a banker.
Worked out purdy good too.
Frat boys used the hearse most weekends
and funerals were confined
mostly to weekdays.

Once the frat boys didn't get back on time
and PK had to load up ole Butch Simms
inna back of Jeb Satterwhite's pickup.
Heck, Butch wouldn't of minded a bit
but the Mrs. was as mad as a box of frogs.

So's when the timing looked close
on gettin' the hearse back
for Sadie Wright's funeral
PK made sure them frat boys
knew he needed it by 1:00 PM sharp.
Well at about five 'til one
hearse come roarin' up
frat boys paid
got in their Corvette
and skedaddled and when PK
opened the back to load up Sadie
there was plenty of evidence that
a beer keg or two had leaked or overflowed
or downright exploded in the hearse.

Well PK had to load her up — no choice
and when Sadie's casket came out
at the graveside it was downright fragrant with
cheap bock beer.
Family on the front row kept sniffing
and frowning with looks of disgust
that just don't belong at funerals
'specially funerals of such a proper lady

as Sadie Wright.
Afterwards BJ
one of the town's most
alcohol-challenged fellas
told PK *Hey pickle me up like that.*
Last mile you ride might as well be pleasant.
Heck that's about how BJ smelled
most of the time anyways.

So's PK had to modify his arrangements
'bout this supplemental source of income
and the return inspection requirement
finally killed it off.

So's I ast him again where he got his money.

Couldn't answer at first 'cause
he's baitin' the hook on one pole
and holdin' the worm for the next pole
between his teeth. Once he got through
with gettin' 'em both baited
he looked up and said
It's a long story and if I told you I'd have to kill you.

Now no matter how long or how interesting
that story was I wasn't no longer officially
interested — not on them terms.

So I changed the subject and reckoned

that the new state trooper
who replaced trooper Blackwell
had done gone and stepped in it
'cause she gave the county judge's
brother-in-law — who she didn't know
was the judge's brother-in-law —
a ticket for drivin' his new John Deere
spraying rig on the highway
and stackin' up traffic all the way back
from NeverDry Creek to his northfork gate.
Coulda gone on county roads
but that woulda tooken longer.
Still new trooper pulled him over
like a common criminal.
Don't reckon the judge
is gonna like some new trooper
pullin' over people in his county
for such things without at least first
checkin' it with him — brother-in-law or no.
Heck farmin' is hard enough around here
without no trooper tellin' you where you can
drive your equipment.

Anyhow I shoulda knowed better.
My Daddy always said
Don't ask a man about his religion
his girlfriend or how he got his money.
I kinda forgot that 'til it was reinforced
by PK's death threat.

Bingo

Me and PK was headed
to the Cow Patty Bingo Field
to see how our fortunes was runnin'
so to speak.
We each had purdy good numbers
and thought this might just be our year.

The bingo field is just north of town
on Ben Hunt's place.
It's right next to the rodeo arena
which is why it's such a first class
Cow Patty Bingo Field.
Bleachers face east towards the rodeo arena
so's the top row is a good seat
for lookin' west to the bingo field.
Ben fenced it square and planted grass
and lets the PTA use it every year for bingo
and now the Presbyterians is usin' it
and the Baptists is thinkin' about it.

So's here's how you play Cow Patty Bingo.
You divide the field into a hunnerd squares
by stripin' ten by ten with lime or chalk.
Then you number the squares and sell 'em
for twenty dollars each.
A thousand dollars goes to the PTA
and a thousand dollars is split
amongst the winners.

So's you turn loose a cow or cows on the field
and whatever squares they decorate
with their patties is the winner.
If it's on the line, both squares win.
Referee's decision is final on liners.
Once't one fell right smack where
27, 28, 37 and 38 meet.
All four winners had to share.

The official PTA Cow Patty Bingo
took some refinin'.
First time they tried it
they used the football field.
Cleanup crew missed one on square 87
and the following Friday night the visiting
team's wideout slipped makin' his cut
on a down-and-out and ball sailed
right over him — was third down, too.
Best defensive play of the year
for the Prosper Prairie Fires.

One year the cows got some bad silage
before they's turned loose on the field
and they really turned loose
and didn't make regular patties.
Had to have a do-over two weeks later and
some folks whose squares had been drizzled
was mighty upset.

And then there's the time Scooter Rogers
tried to rig the game by trainin' his cow to
always graze to the right 'til she hit the fence.
That brought two changes — random drawing
for numbers and random selection
of the game cows.

Decidin' on the right number
of "markers" was hard too.
Even toyed with the idea of a timed event.
But one year — when it was so dry that
the trees was whistlin' for dogs —
they finished the allotted time with
nary a patty and had to go into overtime.
Finally settled on the referee watchin' the cows
and herdin' 'em off the field after four plops.

And then that nerdy Kaplan kid done a study
of all the winning numbers since
Cow Patty Bingo started.
Said certain numbers
seemed to be winnin' more'n others.
Offered to buy 23 and 34 for fifty dollars each
or trade two numbers for 65.
Ginned up quite a bit of tradin' and sellin'
of numbers but the extra money generated
didn't go to the PTA.
First year he sure 'nuff picked
three of the four winners.

Next year he sold a tip sheet
givin' odds on each square winnin'.
People was buyin' the tip sheet
and sellin' numbers
and interest in Cow Patty Bingo
was at an all-time high.
PTA even met to consider sellin' some
squares at a premium the next year
but didn't.
Third year Kaplan got zero out of five
(they's one that was a liner).
Tip sheet wasn't much better next few years
and people quit buyin' it and tradin' tickets
and finally he just give up.

Now it's an official game and a regular event.
Neat thing is that most of the winners
('specially if they's businesses)
give their winnings to the PTA too.
One time The House of Hair had a winning
square and MayBob didn't want
to contribute to the PTA.
*I've contributed $20 every year for ten years
so this is just a return of my money* she said.
But when her business slacked off
for a coupla months she made
a very public donation to the PTA.
PTA was plum grateful for her generosity
and business picked right back up.

So's anyways back to me and PK.
We was sittin' at the top of the bleachers
watchin' this year's bingo game unfold.
PK had 10, right in the corner
and corners is lucky 'cause a stupid cow
can get confused and stay all day in a corner.
and I had 45 and 46
kinda right in the middle.
I was figurin' it was mighty lucky
to have two together.

Cows was wanderin' mostly down in the 70's
when Marva Pitts' silly lapdog
run through the bobbed wire fence
yippin' and yappin' and carryin' on.
Cows flinched and scattered
and when they stopped
the plops for this year was complete.
Me and PK didn't wait around
for the referees to declare the winners.
We could see from the bleachers that
we was shut out again.

Mary's Free Will Café

I was sittin' in Mary's Free Will Café
drinkin' coffee black as thunder.
Mary pulled up a chair and started
chattin' me up about the weather
price of diesel at the co-op
cotton futures and the split
in the Methodists over whether women
should be allowed to be state troopers.

Mary's been runnin' Mary's
for nigh unto twenty years.
Serves the best coffee of anywhere
in the county that's not a campfire.
Doesn't serve evening meals every day
just when she feels like it.
Folks'll call in and say
You cookin' tonight, Mary?
Sometimes she is — sometimes she ain't.
Lotsa folks plan their eatin'
based on her inclination.
When she's a mind to she can chicken-fry
a steak with the best of 'em
but she's always there every morning
for coffee and short order breakfast
and chattin' up the local gossip.

Café only took up Mary's name
'bout fifteen years ago.

Before that her and her husband opened it up
and even though Mary done all the work
he named it for hisownself: Gross' Café
— his name was Ted Gross.
Didn't sound too appealin' for a diner
and folks motorin' through town
mostly just kept on motorin'.

Like I said, Mary was there day and night
and locals always liked her and her coffee
but that lazy SOB Ted almost never
set foot in the place and it was mostly
empty as a dance hall at noon.
Well a coupla years into it
Ted run off with a big ol' gypsy gal
who come to town with a carnival.
She run the ring toss.
'Bout a year later Mary got the circuit judge
to do her a divorce. She felt de-obligated
about the name of the Café.
Changed it to Mary's Free Will Café and
cooks only when she damn well pleases.

So's finally her chattin' gets over to
Buster and Liz Kaplan's son.
Buster (real name is Bolivar — I ain't lyin')
has the Busted Knuckle Garage
and Body Shop south of town.
Him and Liz had a nerdy kid

big ears, big teeth, big glasses
who left for some fancy college in California
and never come back.
Anyways Mary heard that the kid
made a dump truck load o' money
and Mary sorta accidentally overheard Liz say
that he made his money writin' code.
Me and Mary figured he must be
some kinda spy if he's writin' code
and if he's sellin' it for heaps o' money
maybe he's a double spy.
I used his Bingo Tip Sheet a time or two
back there a bit and from what I recollect
he was good with numbers
but he shore didn't look like no spy to me.
If that's the kinda spy we's paying
big bucks for I'm guessin' we has fallen
well below the international standard.

Now I was interested in Mary's take
on the Methodists' problem
'cause Mary ain't no libber and
she had lots o' contact with our local troopers
servin' coffee and sweet rolls every day.
Most everyone thought trooper Blackwell
was sweet on Mary's daughter
but he got transferred to the border.
And the new lady trooper ain't never passed

on coffee at Mary's whenever she's driving
through Prosper 'specially early of a morning.
Well Mary was strangely tongue-tied on the
trooper issue — harder to pin down
than a cricket on a hot griddle.
Said it wasn't her fight
her being a Baptist and all
and troopers both guys and gals
was good sources of gossip
and a steady source of income.

Since she dried up on that subject
I went to anotherwhere — ast her if she ever
changed her mind after she said *Not tonight*.
Funny look tiptoed across her face and
then she realized I meant about her cookin'.
One time, she said, smilin'
with her eyes lookin' to the back of her head.
I been cussed and begged and threatened
but Gol Durn if I don't feel like it, I ain't cookin'.
That's why I call it Mary's Free Will Café.
Onliest time I ever changed was
right after I changed to Free Will.
It was a day or two after changin' signs and
after all the hullabaloo of the Grand Opening.
I was tired, but a good kind of tired.
Phone rang about noon.
You cookin' tonight, Mary?
It was Burt Castor

*never married seldom bathed, always whinin'.
Feller doesn't go to church, doesn't like kids
doesn't tip the waitresses
won't mow his right-of-way
talks more than he listens.
Hell, talks more than he thinks.
Table manners like buzzards on road kill.
And he was about the onliest one in town
didn't come to the Grand Opening.*

So I told him Nope, not cookin' tonight
*before I gave much thought about it.
As the afternoon went on more calls
from more civilized folks and I decide I will cook
so I call him back and tell him.
Made me think:
If I'm gonna go with this free will thing
I have to consult with and follow my heart
'cause your heart might sometimes give you
bad advice but your heart will never lie to you.*

*And shore enough, ol' Burt came
ate by himself in the corner
and when he snuck out that night
he left a fifty dollar tip and a red rose with a card
said* Congratulations on Mary's Free Will Café.

Rose is dried and hangin' on the wall
next to Free Will Mary's first dollar.

Tumbleweeds

Years ago I was on my way to the
Busted Knuckle Garage and Body Shop
needin' some serious help with my pickup.
Buster Kaplan, owner and operator
is a right handy mechanic
a rusty metal artist
a tinkerer and an inventor.
He can make the sickest pickup
purr like a kitten
or the tiredest tractor
roar like a lion.

Way back yonder when everyone brought
their cotton to the gin
in chicken-wire sided trailers
you had to get inside the trailer and sweep
or shovel the last wads of cotton out.
Well Buster invented a Grabber
that picked the trailer plumb up
turned it upside-down, shook it
and got the last scrap of cotton.
Speeded up the ginnin' a right smart
with no more climbin' in and out of trailers.
Trouble was most cotton trailers
was pretty flimsy and Buster's Grabber
shook about every third one apart.
Kinda cancelled out
them advantages I talked about.

As I was saying, I was on my way
to the Busted Knuckle to get Buster
to fix the fender of my pickup.
Don't really care if it's dented or gnarly
but it seems to be scraping the tire
on one side and somethin'
makes a terrible noise whenever I turn right.
All this started Tuesday night when a wild pig
size of a small pony wandered
in front of my right headlight
as it led the rest of my pickup down FM 1853.

So I'm about to the Busted Knuckle
and relief for my squealin' tire when
I sees a bunch of kids pluckin' tumbleweeds
off the bobbed wire fence
and tossin' 'em into a cotton trailer
being towed by none other than PK.
Seems that PK had talked the 4-H Club
into cleaning tumbleweeds off of
the bobbed wire fences as a service project
and he was providin' the cotton trailers
and storin' them tumbleweeds in his barn.
This had been goin' on for weeks
and I ain't never noticed it.
Now I figgered PK was up to something
and I needed to visit with him about it.

Anyways as I worked my way over

so as to get to the Busted Knuckle
making only left turns
I sees Buster out in front
admirin' some of his own work
and it was worth admirin' too.
Buster had painted the new firetruck
that the PVFD had recently swapped for
to replace the one that BJ burned up
overhelpin' at the firehouse.
Seems BJ was cleanin' road tar off the fenders
with gasoline when he accidentally
decided he needed a cigarette.
Almost burned the firehouse down.
Did burn up the firetruck
and with a little help from his friends
allowed BJ to stop smokin'
at least around the firehouse.

So here is this 1972 firetruck,
lookin' all brand new and red —
gold letters and brass fittings.
Buster really outdid hisself on that paint job.
Volunteers couldn't hardly wait for a fire
so they could show it off.

So Buster looks at my fender
says *Whadya hit?*
I says *A hog.*
He says *Where is he?*

never bein' one to overlook roadkill venison.
Well the vultures pretty well took care of it I says.
Too bad says Buster turnin' back to the pickup.
Whenya you need it?
Yesterday.
Don't reckon I can do that
but tomorrow is a possibility.
How much am I lookin' at? I ast
'cause the whole heap ain't worth much.
Value goes up or down
depending on how much gas is in the tank.
Hafta see if I gotta straighten the frame he says.
Just git the fender offen the tire I says
I'll worry about the frame later.

Now I hadta find a way home
and a ride back tomorrow
and who should drive up
but PK and a trailer-load of tumbleweeds.

Turns out PK had moseyed over
to the Busted Knuckle Garage and Body Shop
just to see the new firetruck.
She was sittin' out front
all red and gold and shiny as a snuff can.
Buster had re-worked the pump and
tuned the engine and PVFD number one
was one mighty fine specimen.
What folks didn't know but I did

'cause I'd been down to Mary's
and Mary told me in a most confidential way
was that PK had paid for the new paint job
and workover.
He's good folk like that.

After PK finished admirin' the firetruck
I ast him if I could hitch a ride home
since my pickup was temporarily indisposed
at the Busted Knuckle.
PK said sure so I jumped into the suicide seat.
His dog Ralph — me havin' got his place
jumped in the back.
PK checked the trailer hitch
and got in the driver's side.
He didn't say a word about the load
of tumbleweeds in the trailer
and I wasn't about to.

As soon as we cleared the town limits
of Prosper that trailer begun to tug
and sway and wag the pickup
like Ralphie shaking a dead rattlesnake.
The wind was fierce, the trailer tall
and filled to the brim
and one thing tumbleweeds can do
is catch the wind
so we slithers along the road
barely stayin' between the bar ditches

and I'm wonderin' if PK has any taillights
on this rickety old trailer
but he don't say a word
and I wasn't about to.

So's we git to PK's place and he turns in
drives straight to that big old barn o' his
jumps out, tosses me a pair of gloves
and says *How 'bout helping me sort 'em?*
And we unload them tumbleweeds
into four separate areas where
the barn has been divided.
In one goes tumbleweeds
'bout the size of a basketball
in another goes tumbleweeds 'bout knee high
in another, the big uns 'bout up to your waist
the fourth was for broken, lopsided
or crushed of any size.

PK still never said a word
about what we was doin'
'cept to second-guess or comment on
some of my sizing and sorting choices.
When we was through
PK unhitched the trailer
said *Hop in* and took me home.
Silence filled the cab
but I wasn't about to ask.

Much obliged I said when we got to my place.
You're welcome he said
knowing how I hate the *No problem* response
you get from most folks today.
Thanks for helping me unload.

When PK drove off
without sayin' nothin' more
I had to admit it was
an extreme puzzlement to me.
I cogitated and cogitated and
couldn't come up with no reason
for PK to be collectin' and segregatin'
tumbleweeds. Seemed to me he'd 'bout
cornered the market in tumbleweeds
but far as I know no one missed 'em.

Next day drinkin' coffee at Mary's
I ast her if she knew what the heck
PK was doin' with them tumbleweeds.
When Mary didn't know
we both wondered out loud if livin'
in the outback of Prosper had got to him
and he just rattled a screw loose.
Then one day not much later
ole Brownshirt the UPS man
comes into Mary's, plumb flabbergasted.
What the heck is Mr. Taylor up to he says
shipping tumbleweeds to New York City

and Boston and Chicago?

Like unravelin' a feed sack
one thing led to another
and turns out that PK had set up
and was sellin' tumbleweeds
to big city decorators to paint and stack
and make holiday snowmen.
Made a right smart of money in that endeavor
enough to fund a 4-H scholarship.
He eventually turned the whole project
over to the 4-H to run.
The Ag teacher Mike Sims supervises it
and they make more money every year
than Cow Patty Bingo.
No contest.

MAYDEAN

Me and PK and the boys
was swillin' coffee at Mary's Free Will Café.
On account of the funeral
we was swappin' MayDean Masterson stories.
MayDean was a spinster
lived on her family homestead west of town.
When they dammed Hanson Creek
to make a water supply for Prosper
it split MayDean's place in two
leavin' the house way up on the other side of
the lake from her best pastures
and givin' her most of the shoreline
of the best lake in Shoemaker County.

MayDean purt near never left
the Masterson place.
Had all her groceries and supplies delivered.
Never came to town for church
or even the rodeo.
Only person who saw her regular was
her lawyer Alexander Hamilton Steele.
We call him Ham.
She was about Ham's only client
but fact is she wasn't really the client.
Client was a trust set up for MayDean
by her parents when they passed.
Ham was paid handsomely to represent
the trust and to look after MayDean.

Mostly he just hounded her to cash
the royalty checks that she stacked
on the kitchen table.

One time Barry Don Brooks was delivering
a tractor part that MayDean had ordered
and he smelled a terrible odor
coming from the house.
Figgered MayDean had gone toes up
but she answered his hallo.
Turns out MayDean been bottle-feedin'
an orphaned calf in the house.
When it up and died she just put it
under the bed and forgot about it.
When Barry Don got back to the post office
he called Ham and Ham earned
some of that considerable retainer
convincing MayDean to bring the calf outside
for the vultures and coyotes.

MayDean only runs a few cows
since the lake cut off her best pastures.
She mostly worked them alone 'cause
she run off every cowhand she ever had.
Summer before she disappeared
she was tryin' to pen a coupla strays
in the corral up by her house.
Wasn't havin' much luck.
Critters wouldn't cooperate.

So MayDean, dressed in her granny gown
and cowboy boots, got her shotgun
walked down to the highway
stopped a Greyhound bus
and had the passengers get out
and help her pen her cows.
They hopped right to it and helped her.
It was the onliest thing they coulda did.
She thanked 'em and waved goodbye
as that bus driver loaded up
counted heads and skeedaddled.

Even Barry Don who's might near
her only human contact 'cept Ham
started leavin' her packages at
the mailbox at the end of the road.
And in the fall, there sure weren't no
trick or treatin' at MayDean's.

'Bout that time Mary piped in to remember
that she'd heard that MayDean was one of
them "Christmas kids from Pratt's Camp."
I'm purdy sure MayDean never lived
in Pratt's Camp but she was about
the right age and since her folks owned
the land where Pratt's Camp was
she coulda been there.
The kids that was there
that Christmas was always known as

"the Christmas kids from Pratt's Camp"
to distinguish them
from them who weren't there.
It was the Christmas of 1919.
Pratt's Camp was kinduva temporary
company town for the roustabouts workin'
the Shoemaker County oil boom
and their families — wasn't really a town
just a camp.

One of the oil men thought
it would be a great idea to bring
Santa Claus to the kids of Pratt's Camp.
Was only about a dozen kids
but the gesture was generous.
It was also extravagant
'cause the idea was for Santa Claus
to arrive in a hot air balloon.
With everyone assembled
the balloon drifted over Pratt's Camp
hit a telephone pole, caught fire and
right there in front of
"the Christmas kids from Pratt's Camp"
killed Santa Claus — not just killed him
burned him in that wicker basket
like a batch of campfire popcorn.

Throughout their lives
"the Christmas kids from Pratt's Camp"

got cut a lot of slack — it excused drinkin'
and wild drivin' and petty crime.
I reckon it oughta excuse a dead calf
or a Greyhound holdup too
even 90 or so years removed.
Also might explain why some folks
thought that MayDean might be
a few bricks shy of a load.

Next Mary's daughter Flo chimed in.
In 1957 MayDean bought
a brand new Chevrolet Impala.
She couldn't drive and had nowhere to go.
Never got a license but lookin' back it was
about her midlife so maybe there was a crisis.
Anyhow a few years back MayDean started
hiring Flo who was just a teenager
to drive her to San Angelo
not regular but on random occasions.
Flo says MayDean would always say
she wanted to go to San Angelo
'cause she thought Prince Charles
might be there and she'd like to meet him.
Talked about Prince Charles all the way over
but mostly not on the way back.
That conversation was mostly 'bout
the pitiful price of cattle
and the high price of feed and the
damned motorboats on Hanson Creek Lake.

Onliest trip that car ever made
was to San Angelo and back.
Most of the time it just sat in MayDean's barn
waitin' to go see Prince Charles.

PK always had a soft spot
in his heart for MayDean.
I told you MayDean never came in to Prosper
not even for church but one time
way back all the way when PK's Dad was
preacher at the Prosper Methodist Church
church was strugglin' to find proper classrooms
for a set of kids who was boomin'
(even though oil had long since busted
cotton was marginal as always and
ranchin' was just scratchin' along).
MayDean called PK's dad out to her place
and told him to build a new church.
Gave him land on the edge of town
and told him just to send any bills for
the building to Ham and she would pay them
and he did and she did.
And the Methodists had the most modern church
in town — not fancy
but I reckon if they'd built
a Renaissance cathedral MayDean
woulda never flinched.

Last February when those fierce Northers

come through reminding us all
that there ain't nothing between Prosper
and the North Pole but a bobbed wire fence
Barry Don noticed that MayDean hadn't
picked up her junk mail for several days.
Checked in the house and couldn't find her.
Figgered she wandered off
lookin' for some stray cow.
Sheriff organized a search party.
They scoured the hills and bluffs around
her house down to Hanson Creek Lake.
Didn't find her.
Come spring a fisherman on the lake
way back in one of the sloughs
found a patch of flowery flannel.
Turned out to be MayDean's nightgown
and her boots and shotgun and what was left
of Prosper's oldest character.

PK had the last story of the first pot of coffee.
He got to telling about the funeral
and most particular about the graveside.
Memorial was at Prosper Methodist
as expected. Most people there
had never met MayDean never seen her
came mostly out of curiosity.
But due to the circumstances
casket was closed.

After the service, PK and his crew
from Beloved Rest Cemetery
loaded MayDean into the hearse
and drove out to her place.
Burial wasn't at Beloved Rest
but at a family plot on the highest bluff
on the Masterson spread.
MayDean's folks was buried there —
her parents, grandparents and a few children
and babies that lived a short hard frontier life.

After the crew lowered MayDean's coffin
into its rocky grave and left
PK looked around.
Barry Don was leavin'
and Flo and Ham, too
and there, in the wind and blowin' dust
was a stranger in a dark coat and hat.
Hat was reverently off and in his hands
head bowed.

And then it was just him and PK.
PK sidles up to him and ast *Was you kin?*
No said the stranger
My name is Charles. I'm just a friend.
Got back in his big black car and skeedaddled
down the dirt road to the highway.

ZERO

Did you see that? PK says to me as we sat down
with a cup of Mary's hottest blackest coffee.
Reckon I didn't see whatever **that** was.
So's I just shrug at PK.

That guy paying out at the counter.
I looked over in time to see him
pick up his change with a left hand that
looked like a lobster-claw
— only a thumb and Pinkie —
Pointer, Tall Guy and Ring Finger gone.

Well, I knew right away who it was.
Used to be a skinny kid when him and me
was the same age growin' up.
Now he's got big and old.

You're in the presence of greatness
I says to PK as greatness opened the door
and stepped out into the heat and wind.
That there's Zero Swift.
Onliest farmer in Seco County I reckon
that ever played major league baseball
and the onliest pitcher in the history of ever
to be the winning pitcher in a game
where he didn't even throw a single pitch.

How'd he get that nickname "Zero?" ast PK.

Weren't no nickname I tell him.
His parents named him that straight out.

Swift family lived in the farming community
of Dump 'bout sixty miles northwest of Prosper.
First boy was named Noel
'cause he was born on Christmas.
Second one was named Leon
'cause he was the opposite of his brother
and tag-along came almost twenty years later
a complete surprise and named Zero.
We didn't plan no more kids said his Dad — *Zero!*

Zero practically raised hisself.
The other boys was grown and out of the house.
Parents was as old as grandparents
and not that interested.
He was quite an athlete
most especially quite a pitcher.
Never lost a game in high school.
Pitched seven no-hitters
struck out twenty helpless batters in one game.
Zero was a good name for him
as a high school pitcher.

Drafted by the Chicago White Sox
right out of Dump Consolidated High School
he didn't exactly tear up the minor leagues.
Zero didn't really fit as a name no more

but his teammates called him Zero 'cause
they couldn't come up with a better nickname.
He rode them minor league busses and
ate them minor league hot dogs for seven years.
Every spring, he got his hopes up.
Every summer it was more of the same,
every winter back to work on the farm in Dump.

Then one September
after another roller coaster season in the minors
and seriously thinkin' about quittin' baseball
Zero got his call up to the Show.
Sitting on a major league bench was way better'n
sittin' on a minor league bench
or wrasslin' with a rusty irrigation pump.

So's in the ninth inning
of a meaningless game
near the end of the season
Skipper looked down the bench
and said *Zero, go loosen up.*
By the time he got the nod to enter the game
the White Sox was trailing 4 to 3
with two out and a runner on first.

Musta felt good after all them years
finally standing on a major league mound.
Zero stared at the batter
got the sign from the catcher

and looked over to the runner on first.
In a flash he threw over to first
picked the runner off
and ended the visitor's threat.

The White Sox scored two runs
in the bottom of the ninth and won the game.
Zero was the official winning pitcher
without ever throwing a pitch.
Lots of minor league pitchers
most of 'em, I reckon
never throw a pitch in the Show.
but Zero Swift is surely the onliest one
of that group with a major league **W**
by his name.

That winter Zero stuck his pitching hand
way too far inside a hay baler
that was giving him trouble
and at the end of that fateful day he had
only Pinkie and a mostly opposable thumb
and his major league career was over.

A few years ago Zero built hisself
a pitching mound out behind his barn.
His momma and daddy and Noel and Leon
is gone now but every once in a while
at the end of the day that big old farmer
in grimy overalls and steel-toed boots

climbs up on that mound
closes his eyes and remembers
and with a two-fingered grip
no major leaguer would attempt
throws rocks at the barnyard cat
mostly high and outside so's not to hurt it.

Next time I was to Mary's, PK was already there
sittin' in the corner readin' a book
chucklin' to hisownself.
Whatcha got, a new comic book? I teased him.
Nope. Better'n that. I was over to the
Methodist Church Yard Sale yesterday
I saw this book and bought it for two-bits:
Choosing a Name That Fits.
PK's chestnut mare was about to throw a foal
and he had been worrifying over naming it.
Thought the book might help.

Well he shows me the book and it is a treasure.
It has names that really belong in another time:
Gertrude and Mabel, Elmer and Chester,
people I grew up with
names you've never heard like
Arcineaux and Deltamonte
names as timeless as Mary and Robert
as new as Jayden and Ashley.
Seeing all those names will remind you
of your grade-school sweetheart

your weird scoutmaster
your best and worst stereotypes.
You'll remember names from the past
imagine faces to go with strange new names.
You'll smile and you'll tear up.
Shoot, PK even got a name for the new foal
Mel — in honor of its chestnut mom.
And best of all on the last page
alphabetically-challenged:
Zero.

Froggy McNamara

Me and PK was at Mary's
chewin' on some of her coffee
and recollectin' Froggy McNamara.
Froggy was a man with a distinctive shape
and an equally distinctive voice.
Used to be an auctioneer way back when.
Most people 'round here remember him
though as the best square-dance caller
in Shoemaker County.
He used to sit his wide ass on two chairs
and call dosey-does all night long
new ones, old ones, favorites
'til the dancers hollered "uncle."
I miss his calls.

When Froggy passed
the square-dance club disbanded
and for boot-scootin' they went
to line-dancin' at the library
on third-week-of the-month Saturdays.
Come to think of it Froggy's passing
caused quite a shift here in Prosper.
Line-dancin' at the library became
the favorite activity 'cept maybe Forty-Two
down at Jerry Don's John Deere
or ropin' at the arena
dependin' on who you ast.
I figure line-dancing is so popular because

you don't have to bring a partner
and the gals don't have to wear those puffy
spin skirts that the square dancers all have.
Anyhow line-dancin' is how
Widow Cathcart hooked up with Joe Bob Helms
so I guess their getting hitched is
directly traceable to Froggy's passin'.

'Nother thing I miss about Froggy
is his Walmart hearing aids.
Sometimes at Forty-Two
or at Mary's on chicken-fried steak night
if you heard a chirpin'
it was likely Froggy's hearing aid
screamin' feedback into his ear.
Everyone heard it but Froggy.
He musta just learned to ignore it.
If he wasn't hearin' it
I reckon he needed a more powerful
hearing aid or at least one that fit better.
I miss that chirp.

PK's memories of Froggy
was in a somewhat different vein.
PK allowed that Froggy's funeral
had been his biggest challenge
at Beloved Rest Cemetery
and somehow his biggest failure.
I just naturally figgered it was 'cause of

Froggy's considerable heft.
Everyone in town knew from the viewing
that PK and Jeb Satterwhite
had somehow spliced together
two of their best oak coffins
and folks figgered they musta dug
a two-plot hole to accommodate
Froggy in repose.

I says to PK *That had to 'a been hard.*
Nah says PK *that part was easy.*
Nobody ever knew about the hard part.
This sounded like it might be a good story
so I leaned back, topped off my coffee
and waited for PK's full explanation.

Since they was diggin' a double hole
PK had the boys start early the day before.
Crew was the regulars, the Holt brothers Doug
and Dan — we just called them
Digger One and Digger Two.
Diggin' went pretty good and was uneventful
but when they come back the next morning
the day of the funeral to rig the pulley
for lowerin' the double casket
a skunk had fallen into the hole and was
pacin' around assessin' its predicament.
Even though PK didn't exactly recruit these
diggers from the Honor Society

they knew enough to know that
they had to get that skunk out
before they put Froggy in.
Easiest way woulda been to shoot him
but they knew PK wouldn't approve
and a shot skunk usually sprays
as a final farewell.

Digger One said he heard if you put a blanket
over a skunk's head so's it can't see
it won't spray. Seemed worth a try
and sure enough when they dropped
a blanket over it — no spray.
There was, however, no immediate volunteers
to jump down in that hole and hand him up.
So they rock-paper-scissored
until Digger Two was anointed.
He jumped down
grabbed up the skunk
still wrapped in the blanket.
When he picked it up and put it
over his head to pass it outta the hole
the skunk peed right on him.
Digger Two dropped the skunk.
Skunk sprayed and Digger Two
quickly exited the hole straight up six feet.
Not to be defeated
Digger Two gathered hisself
jumped back down into the hole

covered that skunk with the blanket
and tossed him out.
The skunk ran for the far end
of Beloved Rest Cemetery
but the harm had been done.

And that's how it come to PK's attention:
two diggers stinking to high heaven
and a two-plot hole full of skunk fumes.
PK sent both Diggers home
to burn their clothes and he gave them
each a bottle of ketchup to use
for shower gel and shampoo.
It's the best de-skunk-er ever.

New clothes and a ketchup bath addressed
one problem but the remainin' one
seemed a bit harder and that's where PK
as they say, made a poor decision.

Since striking a match or lighting a candle
can defumigate a bathroom or an outhouse
PK figured a couple of gallons of gasoline
in the hole might sterilize it.
Didn't exactly work but it made
quite a spectacle — a pretty big boom
and a Froggy-sized plume of smoke.
Burned the graveside tent like it was
a cheap Roman candle.

PK had to call up to the church
and cancel the graveside service.
Sent the two Diggers, cleanly dressed
and smellin' slightly like a plate
of Dairy Queen french fries
to the entry of Beloved Rest
to steer people away.
PK apologized to the family
and invited them back
for a graveside service
when the area was less fragrant.
Went pretty well even though lowerin'
that dadoed casket into the two-plot hole
proved to be more challenging
than originally contemplated.

Anyhow we was still rememberin' Froggy
when the newlyweds Jodi and Joe Bob Helms
walked into Mary's and sat down.
They was bustin' with pride over Joe Bob's
new Walmart hearing aids.
Made me smile.
I figgered it wouldn't be too long before
I'd hear the old feedback bug chirpin' again.
Rest in Peace, Froggy.

LOVEY

Shore up that corner post and get a good brace on it

I says to PK as me and him was fixin' fence
down to the north end of my place.
PK didn't know his ass from deep center field
'bout fencing but he was a right good neighbor
and always ready to help.
Settin' posts and stretchin' bobbed wire
ain't no one man job.
Or maybe it is, but it's lots harder
and lonelier that way.

Hand me that come-along I says

and while I was fiddling with it
pinchin' one glove off
droppin' the pliers on my toes
and generally havin' a hard time
PK says *I had an interesting conversation
with Shorty Newsome.* — I says *Oh!
Yessir, he came into Beloved Rest Cemetery
to get plots for him and Lovey.*
What's interesting about that? I ast.
Is they sick or something?
Did Lovey have another vision?
No says PK.
You know Shorty is the frugal one of them two.
He wouldn't pay a nickel to see Jesus ride a unicycle.

Well Shorty wanted a double-decker
— two coffins in one plot.
That's not unheard of
but it's mostly in the pauper's section
where the county is paying the bill.

Then Shorty says You gotta promise me
one thing and in fact I want it in writing.
No matter who dies first, I go on top.
I told him that it would cost extra
hoping to discourage him.
In fact it'll cost more than two plots
where you could be side-by-side.
How much more? says Shorty
When I told him, he reached down into his boot
and brought out a wad of the nastiest
foulest hundred dollar bills you ever saw.
Not only that he reached into his back pocket
and handed me an official legal contract whereas
Beloved Rest agreed to do just as he said.
What's more said Shorty
if I die first and she talks you outta this
I'll come back and haunt you 'til you start diggin'
your own hole.

As I begun to put some tension
on the bobbed wire it seemed to me
that there might be just a little tension
between Shorty and Lovey.

Not really surprising.
They was a real unlikely couple.
Shorty was a simple country cowboy
quiet and leathery no nonsense.
Not exactly the sharpest knife in the drawer
but a solid cowboy.
Lovey (Lovina was her given name
nobody knew Shorty's) was a city gal —
loud and dark — a force of nature.
When she said jump Shorty would
squat down and say *which way* and *how far*.
They met on Shorty's great adventure
to New York City.
To hear him tell she latched on to him
and charmed him and he just
rounded her up like a lost calf
brought her home
and married her.
He was tired of doing his own laundry
cookin' and washin' dishes.
She was tired of New York City.

Hand me them pliers and a couple of staples.

Shortly after they got married
Shorty left the Cowboy Church of Prosper
and they started goin' to that Bethel Prayer
Church on the west side of town.
One Sunday they shows up at church

wearin' red cloth bands around their necks.
Lovey had sewed them on account of a vision
she had about the end of the world comin'.
She told everyone that she wanted some way
for Jesus to identify the true believers
when He come back.
Before long everyone at Bethel
was wearing a red neckband.
Shoot there wasn't nothin' to it.
Looked like a turtleneck without the sweater
but people wanted them
faster than Lovey could make them.
Since the intent was to help Jesus
Lovey couldn't rightly charge for them.
She just give them away.
But when certain Baptists and
Presbyterians around town
started wearin' 'em she realized
she couldn't be sure whether the wearer
was a true believer or not
(although I'm thinkin' Jesus woulda known)
so she started sellin' 'em.

It was a right smart of fun
to watch this thing grow.
One of the girls from Prosper
who was going to college wore one
when she went back after spring break
and all her sorority sisters wanted one like it.

Soon Lovey realized that she could make them
in different colors and styles
and the sororities and then the fraternities
and then other clubs and groups
wanted their own color schemes.
Some of the local cowboys got theirs
made to look like bandanas
so as to not get made fun of.
In the fall customers lined up
to have them made in their school colors.
Booster club at PHS gave them
away at homecoming.

When Lovey started she called them NeckIDs
for her idea of helping Jesus.
The kids at college turned that to nekkids —
saying *Let's go to Prosper and get nekkid.*
Kinda a crude joke and pretty far
from Lovey's original idea.

Give a pull on that come-along while I tag down this wire.

This went on for about two years
growin' like a snowball.
Lovey and Shorty was runnin' around
like banty roosters buyin' material
sewin' special orders and
sellin' everything they made.
Everyone was proud of their NeckID

some folks had a drawer chocked full.
You'd see them at Walmart
at line-dancin' at the rodeo
at every church in town.
Even seen somber solid black ones at funerals.
Lovey got orders from all over the world.
She was busier than a farmer's wife
with three snakes and one hoe.

See if you can plumb up that post over there.
It looks to be leanin' quite a bit.

Then one week in the fall of the third year
things changed and changed in a hurry.
First rip in the britches happened
at Jake's Gas & Junk Food Emporium.
Feller come in late at night
with a black NeckID pulled up under his eyes
and a silver pistol wavin' from his hand and
relieved Jake of a day's worth of cash.
Then the same week a story ran on the
national news that gangs
in Los Angeles, Chicago and New York
was wearing NeckIDs in their colors
so as to identify their own true believers.
And the final straw was when Shorty told
Lovey that he had heard but not confirmed
that Miss October had her photo spread made
wearing a gold NeckID

and next to nothing else.
Lovey began to see that the original plan
for NeckIDs might not be workin'.
One day she fell asleep at her sewing machine
and woke up with a vision
that it was time to stop.
Never made another'n.
Gradually even the faithful in Prosper
begun to leave theirs behind
and today you can hardly find a NeckID
anywhere in Prosper.
Lovey did set aside a red one to be buried in
just in case Jesus needed any help.

Seems like Lovey's vision-generator
sorta burned out after that.
She once't had a dream about the Super Bowl
with exact score and everything
but neither of the teams in her dream
made the playoffs that year
so if it was a vision
it must be for next year or some other.

Well, lookee who's here! It's Marteen.

Marteen Bisbee, an old cowboy that used to
ride with Shorty, had drove up in his pickup.
Marteen sure done his share of fencin' with
Shorty so we commenced talkin'

the finer points of fencin' with him.
After a bit, he carried the conversation
on over to his buddy Shorty.
Said *When Shorty and Lovey got married*
they just moved into that old line shack
that Shorty had down by the river breaks.
That shack is so small that the bunk beds
are still stacked just like when the cowboys used it.
Said *Lovey always sleeps on the top bunk.*
Shakes his head and allows that he
was personally mighty puzzled
as to when Shorty had given up his
long-expressed and vigorously enforced
preference for the top bunk.
Said *That woman's got a spell on him*
and she'll always be on top.

Me and PK just looked at each other
and shook our heads.

Charlotte's Interweb
or
The Last Free-Standing Piggly Wiggly in the State

Me and PK was swigging
today's first cup of Mary's coffee
examining the proposition that
Life is like a chess game —
all the mistakes are there waiting to be made
when in walks Amhad Getar
with his butcher's apron still on.
Amhad is an Indian
not the kind cowboys used to shoot
but from Calcutta or Taj Mahal
or some such place.

Anyhow Amhad sits down
at the booth across the way
and soon Mary joins him
and they are deep in conversation.
From what I can hear over the walls
of the booth Amhad is having
some sort of gripe from blacks
who are wearing bandannas and
wants Mary to get them back in their cells.
Strange conversation, but that's what I heard.

Awhile back Amhad moved to Prosper to

run a Piggly Wiggly franchise grocery store.
A year or two into that venture
with things going pretty well
Piggly Wiggly spit the bit and announced
that it was pulling out of our state.
Amhad didn't chop down the pole with
the big sign on it in his parking lot
just left it where it was.
On the store window he painted
The Getar Store.
For months he got official and legal sounding
letters from Piggly Wiggly corporate
headquarters in New Hampshire
telling him to stop using the sign.
He ignored them.
Said he wasn't using the sign.
It's just sitting out there in his parking lot.

When Walmart moved into town
most of the locally owned stores
just withered and went away.
Not The Getar Store.
Ahmad had good local produce
fresh, custom-cut, grass-fed beef
and loyal customers because
he worked hard, kept the place clean
and if a cowboy was needing groceries or supplies
and trying to hang on 'til payday
or if a roustabout was out of a job

'cause the rigs had moved on
or if a farmer lost a crop for any reason
Amhad kept a small notebook
and let them keep a runnin' tab.
So The Getar Store embraced Prosper
and Prosper embraced it right back.

'Bout a month ago, Charlotte Silsbee was
shopping at the Piggly Wiggly/Getar Store.
Charlotte had just got a new computer.
She had discovered the wonders
and mysteries of the interweb.
Told people she was havin' fun surfin'
right out here on the High Plains.
In fact Charlotte was so fascinated
by the wonders of the interweb
that she up and quit her job at the Post Office
'cause it was cutting into her Facebook time.

Seems like Charlotte and Sadie Allen stopped
in the aisle near the Cheetos and Chicarrones
and Charlotte was telling Sadie that even
though things were pretty tight and she might
have to ask Amhad to run a tab
she had gone on Craig's List to look
for a red sectional couch.

Turns out that one aisle over
near the lentils and the chickpeas

was Jodi Helms sort of over-listening
to the conversation.
Jodi went home and told her husband Joe Bob that
Charlotte had said that somebody named Greg
Zisk had bred some kind of sexual cows.

Well Joe Bob was a regular at the Forty-Two
game down at Jerry Don's John Deere
so next time a game was on he mentioned
to the boys that Jodi said that Charlotte said
that some guy named Gary had a cyst
from having sex with cows.

Jerry Don never looked up and said
Sounds to me like a bunch of Aggies
was having a party.
That pretty much ended the discussion.

Well Amhad had left the Café
and when Mary came with refills
I asked her what was all that about
blacks and bandanas and how was she
supposed to get them in their cells.
She looked at me like I had spoke French
— then a look came across her face
like she had just solved Fermat's Conjecture
and she threw back her head and laughed.

Amhad had asked Mary if he brought over

the bananas that had turned black
could she make banana bread
which she could then sell in the Café
and he could sell in The Getar Store.

Even though she raised some eyebrows
with her Craig's List story
Charlotte still loves the interweb.
Says that her money predicament
is all but over because she met this
real nice Nigerian Prince online
and he is just dyin' to send over to her
six million dollars soon as they get
the arrangements made with her bank.

I'm thinkin' she might have found
one of life's chess game mistakes
and she could be moving into checkmate.

MacGregors of Broken Toe Ranch

Toughest cowboy in Shoemaker County
ain't even a cowboy —
name of Diana MacGregor.
D-Mac can ride, rope, fence, cuss
chew and spit with the best of 'em.
One year or another she's won every event
at the Shoemaker Stampede
even the bulldoggin'.
She's got more and bigger belt buckles than
any other cowboy in or around Prosper
and she's earned them.
She's rode in the summer
when the sun would blister an iron pipe
and in the winter when blue Northers
drift snow against and over
the bobbed wire fence that is all there is
between Prosper and the North Pole.
She's broke her shoulder shoving cows
into a squeezin' chute
broke her leg when her horse spun out
lost her left pinkie droppin' a trailer hitch on it
broke her right hand in a ropin' bight
and crushed her right cheekbone
throwin' a rowdy calf to the ground.
Just normal cowboy stuff.

She's tough, but not rough
not purdy, but closin' time good-lookin'.

In high school she and Monte MacGregor
set some sorta interscholastic record
for versatility and for just showin' up.
D-Mac — known as Diana Winegarden then
before she married Monte —
D-Mac was a cheerleader and
played trombone in the marching band.
Monte was the wiry center
on the football team and he played cornet.
At halftime it was quite a sight
all them band uniforms
D-Mac in her short skirt
and Monte without his helmet
marchin' around tootin' their horns.
PHS couldn't have fielded
a proper band without them.
It was the onliest way it coulda been did.
And after the band finished
D-Mac and Monte was always
holdin' hands until the rest of the team
came back on the field.

D-Mac really cherished her trombone.
Most folks didn't know she kept it
after she went to full-time cowboyin'.
Most folks didn't know
she had a leather scabbard made
so she could carry it on her horse
and almost no one knew she had

another secret about her horn.
Wasn't really a secret
she just didn't never tell nobody.

At least twice a year ranches
in Shoemaker County had roundup.
Usually a posse of riders
would go out on horseback
scour the canyons and the brush
and push the cattle to holdin' pens
for working — mostly de-horn, brand
vaccinate, castrate and cull.
Sometimes it took several outriders
and several trips to get all the strays.

When roundup time came to Broken Toe
riders showed up to help, but D-Mac already
had every one of her cows in the workin' pen
'ceptin' one old droopy-horned Angus heifer
who had lost an eye due to a rattlesnake bite.
Cowboys was moanin' and fussin' about
having to saddle up and ride to the far reaches
of the Broken Toe just to round up
such a sorry excuse for a cow
or to find its sorry buzzard-picked carcass.
It's all right, boys said D-Mac
I'll just get her like I got the others.
With that she walked out to the hill
next to the working pen

sat down on a camp chair
raised her trombone and started playin'
— playin' disemboweled trombone parts
of Sousa marches and Mozart requiems.
Cows in the pens all looked her way
and sidled over to the closest side of the pen
and, sure enough, in a few minutes
you could hear an answering bellow
and shortly old One-Eye sauntered up
like a drunk stumblin' from a bar.
D-Mac is quite a unique cowboy.

That roundup was the first time I had seen
D-Mac and Monte for the longest time
and Monte looked like he had lost half hisself.
Over the years he had filled out and
become a right robust wrangler
but when I saw him he hardly cast a shadow.
Next time I saw D-Mac down to the feed store
I cornered her and asked her straight out
Is Monte sick? Do we need to put him
on our prayer list?
D-Mac smiled and said it all had to do with
them claw-footed Victorian horse troughs.
I think he looks good she said
He was skinny when I met him.
He was skinny when I married him
so I kinda like him skinny.
I understood the second part of the answer

but I circled the first part around in my head
a couple of times and still couldn't see no
connection between Monte
and his scrawny condition
and them horse troughs.

Seems like several years back
D-Mac and Monte salvaged two claw-footed
Victorian cast iron bathtubs from an old
boarding house that was being torn down.
Put them side by side in the yard
on the west side of their house.
Figgered to use them as horse troughs
for horses who had free roam of the yard.
But one day, on a total lark
Monte cleaned 'em up and come sunset
they climbed in for a relaxing bath
right there in the back yard.
It kinda became a habit for them
a quiet private happy hour.
After a long hot day they would climb in
with nothing on but their cowboy hats and
maybe sunglasses, drink a beer and talk
about the weather, cattle and grain futures
cost of cubes, the encroachment of civilization
on the Amazon rainforest or whatever
serial killer was making the current news.
Sometimes they even got out their horns
and sat there laughing and playing marches

but mostly they just soaked there
side-by-side, holdin' hands and watchin'
the sun set over the Broken Toe Ranch.

One day D-Mac came in late from changin'
the sucker rod on a cranky windmill.
She went out back and saw that Monte
was already in the tub nursin' a beer.
Hon he said *I need your help. I'm stuck!*
It was a time when Monte wasn't near
as slim as he used to be or is now.
In fact he had gone from slim to svelte
to husky to robust right on up to portly
and beyond.
D-Mac sorta snorted.
No he said *I ain't joshing. I'm stuck.*
Can't wiggle. Can't get out.

D-Mac seen he was serious
so they both started workin' on solutions
for this awkward moment.
First thing they tried was bacon grease
from the pantry of the chuck wagon.
Made a mess — and didn't really help.
Next D-Mac got Monte some leather gloves.
Then she brought one of the horses into the yard
handed Monte one end of her best rope
looped the other over the saddle horn
and walked her horse slowly away.

Didn't exactly suck Monte outta the tub.
In fact the first thing that happened was
the back end of the tub come up in the air.
Monte hung on, but then the tub started
to swing from side to side.
Monte eventually let go
got a rope burn where he couldn't discuss
the tub fell over on its side and
Monte was dumped out on the ground
like a jello salad on a picnic platter.
Dirty, covered with bacon grease
and water and sticker burrs
naked except for a pair of leather work gloves
Monte uncurled hisself
put his hat back on and picked up his beer.
Don't say nothing he said as he
stomped off to the house
Don't say nothing.

Monte went on a diet.
Went from a raging omnivore to a paleo
non-fat, low carb, sticks and twigs fanatic.
Didn't stop 'til his belt wouldn't
hold up his jeans and chaps.
Got downright trim —
thinner than a farmer's wallet.

And then him and D-Mac
got back to their daily happy hour

sittin' and soakin', drinkin' beer and laughin'
after all these years, best friends
sittin' side-by-side in claw-footed tubs
watchin' the sun set — still holdin' hands.

BJ'S DOG, CHARLIE

Hadn't seen PK this excited since
he bought Beloved Rest Cemetery.
Said he had a visitor coming all the way from
London England, his financial advisor.
PK says he wants me to help him
show her all the essential sights of Prosper.
Shouldn't be too hard especially since she
allowed she wanted to see pump jacks
cowboys and cotton gins and we got plenty
of all of those around here.

Samantha Thoroughgood was her name.
PK called her Sam. Nice enough lady
but a tad pale, a tad skinny
and a tad uptight for my particular tastes.

Well we showed her a whole field
of pump jacks — got up real close to one.
She hardly believed us when we told her
that the fraternity boys sometimes
come over at night (possibly a little drunk)
and ride them like broncos.

Sam like to fell over when she saw a cowboy
pushin' a shopping cart in Walmart
with his spurs on and his hat off —
his forehead and the top of his head as pink
as a baby's butt above his brown leathery face.

Farmers at the co-op
each holding on to his spitting cup
some wearing overalls older than Sam
got up from their computer screens where
they were trying to milk every last penny
from next fall's crop and shook their heads
when she commenced to talk cotton futures
and hedging strategies with them.

Highlight of her week was to be Saturday's
Shoemaker County Stampede Rodeo.
So Friday night we ended up at Mary's
where PK ordered Sam a chicken-fried steak
and it came out big as a saddle blanket
hangin' over the sides of the plate
a regular playa lake of cream gravy.
Sam just stared at it before gamely diggin' in.
Dinner talk between Sam and PK was
downright weird — they got to talkin' stocks
and bonds and IPO's and ETF's and
derivatives and even more gobbledygook.

I was about to nod off when I heard Sam
say something about belt buckles.
Her fascination with cowboys
had zeroed in on belt buckles.
Sam had seen Shorty Newsome's belt buckle
when him and Lovey came in for dinner
and she declared it the biggest belt buckle

she had ever seen.
Why that ain't nothing I told her.
It only looks big on Shorty.
Let's go on over to 'Tippers and by midnight
we'll see at least three bigger'n that
or I'll buy the drinks.
If we see more, you buy.

She seemed up to that challenge
but what Sam didn't know was that
the semi-finals of the Shoemaker
County Stampede Rodeo was tonight
and after it was over 'Tippers would fill up
with cowboys and belt buckles of all sizes.

So we adjourned to 'Tippers
found a place in the corner and
started a slow process of getting acquainted
with a passel of Lone Star long necks.
PK asked Donny to bring Sam's
from the back so it wouldn't be cold.
She smiled in appreciation.

At the bar was BJ, a regular
most likely the most regular
and at his feet was a sheepdog
layin' quietly with one eye open
and both ears on alert.
How come they let that dog in here? ast Sam.

That's Charlie, BJ's service dog I says.
Looks like a sheep dog to me.
*Usta be 'til he got some special training
now he's a service dog.*
OK says Sam raising her long neck
*tell me **that** story.*

Well I says *gotta back up about two years.
One night Donny was fixin' to close 'Tippers.
Made last call, served last round
and BJ was the onliest one hangin' around.
Donny ushered BJ out the door and
commenced his cleaning-up closing-up things.
So 'bout half an hour after he sent BJ packin'
Donny steps out into the parking lot
and there is BJ's car still sittin' there.
And sittin' in the back seat on the driver's side
is BJ sobbin' and caterwaulin'*
head in his hands.

Donny ast BJ *How come you ain't gone home?*
Cain't says BJ *somebody stole my steering wheel.*

For a long time after that
BJ was banned from 'Tippers.
Then him and Donny had a summit
and after a new arrangement was made
BJ was a regular again.
But the onliest way Donny will let

BJ come into 'Tippers is if Charlie is with him.
Charlie mostly just lays on the floor
under BJ's stool, but after three beers
or if BJ slurs even one word
or if he stumbles on the way to the bathroom
Charlie barks once and, if necessary
latches onto BJ's pants leg
and drags him outta 'Tippers.

Hadn't no more than said that
like it was some kinda signal
BJ waves his hand and hollers
One more, Donny.
Donny hardly looked up.
Charlie perked up and barked.
BJ said *Dang it,* settled his tab and him and
Charlie walked out the door to his pickup.
No one can steal his steering wheel now.

Just about the time BJ and Charlie was exitin'
in comes the crowd from the rodeo.
in comes belt buckles big, bigger
and bigger'n that.
Rodeo trophy belt buckles
NRA belt buckles
belt buckles with initials
belt buckles with flags
belt buckles with praying cowboys
belt buckles with silhouettes

of nekkid cowgirls
you could tell they was cowgirls
'cause they had hats and boots on.
Silver, brass, bronze, even gold
most were smaller than a hubcap
but all put Shorty Newsome's to shame.

My treat says Sam
after the first wave of rodeors came in.
And we settled the tab
before Charlie had to drag us out.

RUMOR MILL

PK missed Wednesday night's Forty-Two
game down at Jerry Don's John Deere.
He was takin' Sam his financial advisor
to Dallas to catch her plane back to London
makin' him and Sam — mostly Sam
fair game and a topic of conversation.

It was reported that folks at Mary's
loved Sam's accent and her
tailored "sporting clothes."
Donny and the guys down at 'Tippers
were reportedly still talkin' about
how she preferred her longnecks
room temperature, not frosty.
Folks at the co-op were still chewin' on her
off-hand calculation that their cotton prices
would be strong for the next couple of years
because unusual weather and political unrest
had pretty well messed up Egypt's ability
to plant and raise its long-staple cotton crop.
Jerry Don got lots of nods and a few chuckles
when he reckoned that Prosper farmers
managed pretty well with their own share
of weird weather and political unrest.

Fillin' in for PK at the main table
was Mike Sims the Ag teacher.
Mike — most people called him Coach —

often came and just sat and watched.
But when there was an opening
at the main table he sat right down
and more than held his own.

Mike Sims was far and away without a doubt
the best Ag teacher we ever had in Prosper.
He organized and supervised the 4-H club.
He coached the Meat Judging Team
the Soils and Grasses Team
the Range Management Team
the Diesel Troubleshooting Team
and the Chess Team.
And Prosper was a threat
to go to State in any one or all of them
'specially Meat Judging.

But aside from all that teachin' and coachin'
he was a loner and a kind of a cypher.
No one could figure out what all he did
out at his home place.
There was lights on 'til all hours
strange smells coming from his barn
and last spring he built a humongous
greenhouse just north of the main house.
Didn't order seeds or plants
from the feed store or the co-op
but you could see something was growing
if you drove past his place

when the sun was setting
behind the greenhouse.

After a few games and plenty of talk
about Sam and PK and other absentees
somebody just straight up and ast Mike
Whatcha growing in the greenhouse, Coach?
Mike looked up from his dominos
grinnin' like a possum eating persimmons.
Oh let's just say it's something unusual for this area.
Well we'd already figured he wasn't growin'
cotton or sorghum or sunflowers
or cattle for that matter
so that really wasn't very helpful
but he didn't seemed inclined to elaborate
and since Jerry Don had just bid eighty-four
the subject was dropped while everyone turned
their undivided attention to
what tile to keep for the last trick.

Now, Prosper is fertile ground for rumors
as well as crops and the Forty-Two game
was close behind The House of Hair
as the starting point for most of 'em.
When you leave a mystery hanging out there
like Coach just did you can imagine
what people started to imagine
was growing right there in their backyard.
So speculation became gossip

and gossip became rumors
and rumors became fact.
Nobody knows exactly who done it
but eventually somebody tipped off the DEA
and with warrant in hand and
Sheriff Posey taggin' sheepishly along
five federal agents in black body armor
swooped down on Coach Sims' place
and confronted him in his greenhouse.
Coach was downright accommodating
Come right on in, boys.
Have yourselves a look around.

Growing and thriving on trellises was a plant
that none of the officers recognized.
Not marijuana the feds said *What the hell is this?*
What you growin' here, Coach? ast Sheriff Posey.
Hops says Coach Sims *just old-fashioned hops.*
Growing my own to freshen my home-brew beer.
One of the feds says
We'll just take a sample back to the lab.
The beer ast Coach *or the plants?*

They didn't think that was all that funny.
Rather have a Schlitz Light said one.
Shoot said Coach Sims
I could feed my horse barley
and he would piss better beer than that.

As you might expect word of the raid
filtered back through the rumor mill.
Most folks was ashamed 'bout what
they had allowed themselves
to think about Coach Sims.
It don't take a very big person
to carry a grudge
but Coach Sims is big enough to let it all go.
Luckily he has a sense of humor
and a forgivin' heart.
And eventually the whole incident
was recast and re-told as an example
of the federal government run amok.

And for a couple of years
farmers and folks at the co-op
watchin' cotton futures
on their computer screens
cursed the weather
cursed the politicians
and hoorayed the price of cotton
raisin' their icy longnecks
to that English gal, Sam.

Nature or Nurture

PK and me was sittin' quietly
lookin' into the black hole
that was a cup of Mary's coffee
but the boys in the next booth
was mighty riled up and loud.
I couldn't tell if Mary was tryin'
to soothe them or egg them on
but she was sayin' that it was mostly
the weak-minded and susceptible —
teenage girls and farmers' wives —
who was being affected.

I said to myself (and only myself)
that my experience is that them particular
groups is anything but weak-minded
or susceptible for that matter.

It ain't natural said one of the boys
It ain't what God intended.
I'm not so sure that some folks
ain't just born that way said another
or just pre-supposed to get that way.
Third fella said *I heard that Jerry Don said*
that he'd been told that Dub's wife come in
and announced that ***she's*** *one.*
This is a crisis and it can all be traced back
to one person — MayBob Holley.
This was beginning to sound

a little like a lynch mob
so I stuck my head around the
corner of the booth and said
Hold on, boys. It's not that bigguva deal.
It's a personal matter and private.
And they ain't hurtin' anybody PK chimed in
It won't affect you unless you let it
and MayBob can't help it.
She is who she is and we all know
she's an important part of the community
and a dues paying member of
the Chamber of Commerce.

That was true, but everyone also knew
from the first day she moved to Prosper
that MayBob Holley was a bubble
or two off plumb.
After all she was young
she was beautiful
she was a vegetarian
she had a purple streak in her hair
and she moved to Prosper voluntarily.

MayBob opened up her salon on Broadway
next to the Bethel Prayer Church.
Called it MayBob's.
Homemade sign out front.
Several months later Bethel put up a sign
that says House of Prayer.

Following week MayBob takes down
her MayBob's sign and puts one up
that says House of Hair
handmade but same size
and color and kinda letterin' as Bethel.
Some thought that was funny
House of Hair — House of Prayer.
Some thought it was blasphemous.
Caused quite a stir.
People would come from all over
to take a picture side by side
with them two signs which was
side by side with each other.
Bethels liked the attention and
mighta growed the congregation 'cause of it.
Seemed to help MayBob's business too.

First thing people in Prosper do when
someone moves to town
is to ask what church they go to.
Kinda helps them assess just
what kinda person this newcomer might be.
Also since Prosper has
shrunk so much over the years
and all the churches keep on keepin' on
Prosper is seriously over-churched.
So if a church can lasso a newcomer
before anyone else does
they up their own chances of survival.

MayBob didn't join any church right away.
She tested each one — givin' one Sunday
to one and the next Sunday to another.
Same for Wednesday night Bible study
and Friday potlucks but her business instincts
kicked in when she realized that if she kept
the House of Hair open on Sunday
customers could get their hair done
while husbands were watching football on TV.
Suited the customers, suited the husbands
and pretty much suited the churches
who didn't know exactly what to do with
a purple-haired congregant no matter
how pretty or how savvy or how nice she was.
Built up her business right smart.
Before long most every teenage girl
and farmer's wife was a customer of MayBob's
down at the House of Hair.

That's why it had such an impact
when she came out.

At first she just told a few customers she felt
close to and who she thought might share
her values or at least be sympathetic.
But then she started to say it loud
and say it proud *I'm no longer a vegetarian.*
I'm a vegan.

Some folks in Prosper didn't know
exactly what that meant.
When Mozelle Tinker told her husband
she was a vegan he said *You can't be.*
You're married and got two kids.
But when her customers considered MayBob's
beautiful skin, luscious hair, enviable figure and
energetic health Prosper slowly edged toward
being the most vegan town
in the heart of ranching country.

Mary's Free Will Café added
vegan choices to its menu
even got a tofu-based chicken-fried steak.
It ain't chicken, it ain't fried, and it ain't steak
but I hear Mary cooks it real scrumpy.
Some gal told her *Mary, this tofu steak is to die for.*
Mary said *Thanks, darlin'*
but you are in the no-dyin' section.
Kinda summed it up.

A motion was even made to add
a Broccoli and Cauliflower Division
to the Campfire Calf Fry Cook-off
at the Shoemaker County Stampede.
It was narrowly defeated after someone wisely
called for a secret ballot vote.

But the ugliest incident from all this

was when the county clerk became such a
devout ethical vegan that she refused
to issue hunting and fishing licenses
because they were contrary to her beliefs.
With dove season comin' up some folks
were madder than a peach orchard hog.
Most folks thought she was just like
all of our other politicians —
wide butt and narrow mind.
Lotsa folks thought she should have resigned
if she couldn't perform the duties of her office
but the judge talked her into lettin' her assistants
do the issuin' of the licenses
and all went back to normal.

One thing I had been right about
talkin' to the boys at Mary's that morning.
Over time it did for the most part go away.
But I guess it's kinda ironical
that one lasting effect may be that those
who did hang on and continued as vegan
will likely live healthier and longer
and delay their candidacy and admission
to PK's Beloved Rest Cemetery.

Coach Tom's Laundry

Me and PK was sippin' coffee
down at Mary's Free Will Café.
PK was starin' in his cup
deep in thought tryin' to figure out
how many Super Bowls the Cowboys
woulda won if they had had
a competent general manager
so he didn't see the guy come in and sit
in the booth at the far end of the room.
I knew the guy wasn't from around here
'cause he was wearin' loafers instead of boots
and he wasn't wearin' any socks
and anyways I know everyone
from around Prosper and Shoemaker County.

He was talkin' to hisself when he came in
he was talkin' to hisself when he sat down
and he was talkin' to hisself when Mary
went over, smiled at him, howdied him
and when he turned his cup over filled it up
with her ebony elixir thick black java.

Now we got a fella around here who knows
a great deal about talkin' to hisself
BJ, the recently reformed town drunk.
Back before Charlie his service dog
pretty much single-handedly
or really four-pawedly sobered him up

BJ was regularly seen walkin' around town
talkin' to hisself
sometimes lecturin' hisself
sometimes comparing notes
sometimes even arguin' with hisself.

One time Donny the barkeep at 'Tipper's
at the request of a concerned customer
had to go into the restroom and talk BJ
out of invitin' the fella he saw in the mirror
and at whom he was shakin' his finger
menacingly out into the parking lot
to settle a very heated argument
he was havin' with hisself.

BJ's semi-sobriety pretty much changed that.
After Donny and BJ and Charlie
worked out their deal whereby Charlie
shall we say reined in BJ's drinking
BJ still walks around talking to hisself
but now we all know he is really talking
to Charlie who trots along tryin' to
look interested in the conversation.

The target of BJ's conversations changed
but one thing that semi-sobriety didn't change
that many around here fervently wished it woulda
was BJ's habits with respect to
his dirty clothes and laundry day.

Most folks from Prosper and hereabouts
who don't have their own washing machine
do their clothes washin' and gossipin'
down at Coach Tom's Laundry.
BJ was no exception.
Onliest thing is that BJ
who must have been raised by wolves
had a unique way of doin' his laundry.
Arrivin' with a red duffle bag full of dirties
was not much different from everybody else.
It's just that in loadin' the machines
he would start with the duffle
dump its contents and then proceed
to take off his shirt, undershirt, boots
(which he would set carefully aside)
socks and pants from which he removed
his billfold, his keys, his belt
and his silver flask
so when the machines were all loaded up
he was simply standin' there
in his tidy whiteys with nowhere
to put his small silver flask
but tucked in the back in the waistband
in his plumber's crease.
It's just a good thing that he had
at least two pairs of jockey shorts.

As you can imagine this curious ritual
generally cleared out the laundromat.

Coach Tom, a retired schoolteacher
who bought the laundromat for extra income
eventually asked BJ not to wash
quite so many clothes at one time
but BJ wasn't one to grasp subtlety
and anyways he was in his forgetful phase
so most of the unwashed of Shoemaker County
just learned to avoid Coach Tom's Laundry
when BJ came to town luggin' his red duffle
over his shoulder like Santa Claus.

Some people were placin' odds that BJ's
laundry routine would change
with his new condition
but in a short time the limits of BJ's semi-sobriety
were on full and glorious display.
Sadie Day was just gettin' her laundry
out of the washers and into the dryers
when BJ and Charlie sauntered in.
Sadie had been one of the most fervent in
hopin' that BJ's laundry routine
would drastically change.
She even prayed for it as part
of her concern for BJ's salvation
but in her heart she knew
what was fixin' to happen
when she saw that red duffle.
So she gathered damp clothes from the dryers
as fast as she could

and departed Coach Tom's Laundry.
Far as I can tell she said afterwards
the only thing that's changed is
he didn't have to reach to his waistband behind
because he didn't have a flask.

Any rate the stranger in Mary's
was still talkin' to hisself and gesturin'
generally ignorin' everybody
and everything around him
lookin' to me like he might be seriously
disconnected from reality
when PK finally looks up and assesses
the solitary chatterbox and says to me
It's only Bluetooth. He's got Bluetooth.

I don't reckon I know
nothing about this fella's dentistry
and I don't know how PK could even see
his teeth from way across the room
but I was greatly relieved when the stranger
stepped outside to finish a monologue
that was **way** too loud and **way too personal**
and almost as pleased to see him return
calm, quiet and composed
howdy everyone in the place
and strike up a normal conversation
with Mary when she came to refill his cup

like whatever demons that had needed his
attention had folded their tents
like Arabs and, as silently, slipped away.

NIGHTHORSE ROUNDUP

What's going on over there? ast PK
pointing to a large table
at the other end of Mary's Free Will Café.
Hunkered around the table was a buncha
youngsters all bandanas and spurs and hats
and some crusty old cowboys
also with spurs and bandanas
pink slick heads shining as their hats
filled Mary's hat rack.

Oh, that's the Nighthorse Cavalry I says
*Rememberin' Nighthorse Roundups past
and gettin' ready for the Stampede.*
Truth be known it fit right in
to where me and PK had been ruminatin'
that very morning before the crowd come in.
We had been chewin' on
some of Mary's best eye-openin' coffee
tryin' to decide whether the next generation
was goin' to be our ruination or our salvation.
I voted salvation because of things like
Nighthorse Roundup.

One thing you don't never hear in Prosper
is kids saying *What can I do? I'm bored.*
Regular chores and the rhythm
of farming and ranching generally
takes care of any issues in that regard.

School sports get some time and have a
familiar rhythm — basketball in the Spring
baseball in the Summer, football in the Fall
but in the Winter when things slow down
there are activities unique to Prosper
and the crown jewel of those activities
is Nighthorse Roundup.

PK allowed aloud that Mary's coffee
tastes even better in the Winter when
the days are short and the wind turns blue.
That's the time to fire up the coffee I says
and saddle up the Nighthorse Cavalry.
What's the Nighthorse Cavalry? ast PK
and what's the Nighthorse Roundup?

Far as I know Prosper is the onliest town
as has a Nighthorse Cavalry and
the onliest activity for the Nighthorse Cavalry
besides leading the Grand Entry parade
at the Shoemaker County Stampede Rodeo
is to organize and execute the annual ritual
of Nighthorse Roundup.

Nighthorse Roundup starts
with the idea of a nighthorse.
Back in the open range days when cattle were
driven to markets far away, each cowboy
sought out at least one nighthorse —

one that could see better at night than others
and who was especially sure-footed
traits that came in handy to keep the herd
together at night when nightrider duty
was drawn and the moon was less than full.
Nighthorse Roundup harkens to that past.
No matter what the weather
no matter how deep the snow
the competition takes place on the darkest night
of the year — the New Moon of December.
Shoemaker County has no city lights to speak of
and the range at night can be as black
as a cup of Mary's leftover coffee.

Nighthorse Roundup is almost
as much like a rite of passage or initiation
into a secret society as it is a sport.
Each year six youngsters, ages nine to twelve
are chosen by the Nighthorse Cavalry.
Ben Hunt has sixteen sections of land
smack in the middle of his river ranch
that's fenced along the surveyed section lines
four miles along each side
ten thousand two hundred forty acres.
Toward sunset the contestants
and their nighthorses are escorted
to the southeast corner of the tract
by four seasoned cowboys
from nearby ranches

all members of the Nighthorse Cavalry.
They make a cowboy campfire
cook a cowboy dinner
and tell stories about cowboyin'
and their ranching heritage.
The cowboys are grizzled
and long in the tooth.
None of them is old enough
to have actually driven cattle
across vast stretches of unfenced prairie
but their grandfathers did
and the stories are rich
and the food is good
and the unspoken purpose
is to let the night
get darker and darker.

Finally the campfire will have burned down
to a few embers and it is time.
The contestants are divided
into two teams of three.
They saddle their horses in the darkness
and ride slowly northwest along the imaginary
diagonal of this tract toward
the opposite corner of the square
no compasses, stars only on the darkest night.
At the same time cowboys in the corners
of the tract to the left and right
release two longhorn steers

with cowbells around their necks.
The object of the competition is to find
and herd the two longhorns assigned
to your team and push them to a holding pen
in the corner opposite the starting place.

Riding in pitch black
through mesquite, cactus and cedar
listening for the clanging
of cowbells requires intense concentration.
Pushing longhorns through that brush and
through the river breaks requires teamwork
excellent horsemanship and hopefully
a good nighthorse.

When both teams successfully bring their
steers to the appointed spot and pen them
four different cowpokes greet them
build a campfire and match tales
of adventure from the contestants
story for story.
A short night's restless sleep
with saddles for pillows usually
wraps up the competition.

Now last year's match was rather unusual
and I reckon that recollecting it is probably
the center of the whooping and hollering
going on across the room.

One of last year's teams had already
brought in both of its longhorns and
corralled them in the holding pen.
The team included the MacGregor twins
who were raised on horseback and
who had two of the best nighthorses
in the county, Radar and Batgirl.
Sorta expected them to do well.
But for the longest time after they arrived
there was no sign of the other team.
No one could even hear approaching cowbells.

The MacGregor team was helping with the
campfire and coffee and fixin' to gloat
over a record winning margin
when the other team finally
appeared in the clearing.
At first there were just two riders
with the two longhorns and then
from the darkness they all heard
galloping hooves
and riding into the light of the campfire
was the youngest and smallest contestant
Sunny Rogers riding her nighthorse, Jedi
racing behind a shaggy wild-eyed buffalo.
Lookee what I found she yelled
as they neared the campfire.
Now the buffalo either had no fear
or was so crazed with fear

that he took off straight for
the campfire and the coffee.
Cowpokes scattered like quail
as he ran right through the campfire.
It erupted like Fourth of July and
the coffee pot clanged off into the darkness.
When the dust and smoke and boiling coffee
had settled and everyone had checked
to see if they were alright
and all systems pretty much checked out
they penned the longhorns and listened
as the buffalo charged off into the night.

Senior cowboy got everyone together.
Must be a fence down between us and
the pasture where Ben keeps his buffalo herd.
We'd better fix it.
So one seasoned cowboy and the only
non-MacGregor from the first team back
started up the fence searchin' for the gap
and the rest of the crew fanned out
to look for the buffalo.
Couldn't none of them did any of this
without a nighthorse.
Towards dawn the line riders found where
a tree had fallen across the fence.
Outriders weren't so lucky and after daylight
they had to call in Ben's helicopter
to locate the old bull.

It was a crazy end to the adventure.

These weren't the first or the only
Nighthorse Roundup contestants to say
That was the best night ever!
And I reckon that's what sport
and life is all about.

Frank Bonner, in Memoriam

When Mary brought me the first cup
of the day she said that the Free Will Café
had been open twenty years.
We calculated that meant that
I'd had the day's first cup of her coffee
roughly 7,305 times 'cept for
the few times PK beat me.
I figgered about nine hundred gallons
or roughly three and a half tons of coffee
not even countin' my refills.
And here I am, not a pound heavier
and my kidneys still functionin'.
Couldn't wait to lay all that on PK
who had had a few first-cups-of-the-day
around 2,500 seconds and no tellin'
how many refills hisveryownself.

I knew PK would be late for today's cup
on accounta he had to meet
with Frank Bonner's widow Bonnie.
Frank had just passed on Saturday night.
The Bonners were a rather unique couple
even for Prosper.
Each one of them had been divorced twice
and married three times
and that was only with each other.
They married, divorced
got back together and married again

divorced again and then re-married
kind of a light switch marriage
on and off, on and off.

Once when Bonnie called Frank to come get
her down at the sheriff's office
because the sheriff had determined
that she was too intoxicated to
continue to try to drive herself home
the sheriff wouldn't let Frank take her
even though he was stone cold sober
because she had a restraining order
out on him that wouldn't allow him
within five hundred feet of her.

Frank Bonner was a mostly good man.
He was sorta Prosper's version of a picker.
Made his living buyin' and sellin' things.
Started by gatherin' inventory
in various city dumps
stuff people had tossed out back
didn't want no more.
He was a genius at re-purposin' —
horse troughs to bathtubs and vice versa
plowshares to platters
ice-boxes to bars
old barnwood to furniture.
And with such a low cost of inventory
he actually did right well.

Eventually Bonner started goin' to folks
and askin' if they really wanted
that rusty implement or crumblin' barn
or obsolete cotton trailer out back.
Gathered lots of free and low-cost stuff
that way — but occasionally he started
collectin' things before people
were officially through with them.
Served three years in the pokey for that.
I think it was between marriages to Bonnie.

Anyhow I figure it was a good thing
for PK and Beloved Rest Cemetery
that one of the times they was married
and gettin' along and Bonner's pickin'
business was workin' out
they came in and pre-paid Beloved Rest
for a plot and two plain ole vanilla funerals.
It was a good thing because they were
as PK himself would say
so cheap they wouldn't give a nickel
to see Abraham Lincoln ride a unicycle.
(I cleaned that up a little, myself).

So Mary and I were discussin' the weather
the state of the cotton crop and just what
economic sanctions might be effective against
North Korea when in walked PK
just a shakin' his head.

After he sat down and Mary poured
he shook his head again and says
Cheapest widow I ever saw.
I says *I thought they was pre-paid!*
Oh they're pre-paid he said
but there are a few things
not covered by that package.
One is the obituary in the Prosper Weekly News
(which we called the Weekly Reader).
I negotiated a good rate at the paper.
It's only one dollar per word
minimum of five words
after a hundred it's free.
I told her that some folks might not realize
Bonner was gone and she could memorialize
his colorful life, but Bonnie still balked.
She pondered on it for a spell and then
the obituary she scratched out reads:

Bonner died. Pickup for sale.

Guess widow Bonner didn't have time
or inclination to do much memorializin'.

Archie

When PK told his story about Archie
this morning my brain went way back
to a conversation we had
at this very booth
three or four years ago.

Archie died PK said back then
and folks want him buried at Beloved Rest.
I don't think I can do it he said.
It wouldn't be right.
Wouldn't be respectful.
But he's already got a plot I pointed out that day
right between the Gardner twins, Gretchen and Gail.
You know they weren't twins said PK
and according to the records of Beloved Rest
the middle plot is for their brother Archimedes.
Their brother was named Gordon I said
and he never came back from WWII.
Archimedes is Archie.
But Archie is a parrot says PK.
True I remember sayin' *but Archie was all the*
family that those Gardner spinsters had.
Well, said PK as he drew another swig of
Mary's dark roast, near-campfire coffee
I still gotta think on this.

The Gardner family — particularly
Miss Gretchen and Miss Gail

has been wrapped up
in the history of Prosper for a long time.
Seven Gardners arrived in Prosper in the fall
of 1929 — Momma and Poppa, two girls and
the triplets, Gordon, Gretchen and Gail.
Rented out an old line shack
down by the rail yard.
Poppa tried his hand at share-croppin'
some of BJ's scrubby land south of town.
In a coupla years Momma and Poppa decided
to keep moving west.
The triplets, all of fifteen years old
and full of piss and vinegar,
said they were tired of moving
and would stay in Prosper.
Went back and forth until one day
Momma and Poppa loaded up the two girls
and left the triplets standing at the curb.
Never came back — never called back.
Triplets never heard from them again.
Triplets just stood there, watched 'em go —
jaws set, no tears and then went about
figurin' how to make it work.

Prosper may be a small town
but it has a big heart.
And the Gardner triplets had a strong will.
Gretchen and Gail got jobs at the Piggly Wiggly
stockin' and checkin' and sackin'

and carryin' out groceries.
Gordon did fence mendin' and
lawn mowin' and paintin'
and washed dishes
at the local diner on the weekends.
Them orphan kids had more parents lookin'
after them from a distance than
Carter had liver pills.
They never missed a Sunday at church
and graduated first third and fifth
in their high school class.
Then someone most likely hard-headed
soft-hearted Maydean Masterson
paid for them to go to teachers college.

After college, Gretchen and Gail
came back to Prosper.
Miss Gretchen taught English
and Miss Gail taught math
in the Prosper schools for sixty-four years.
Almost everyone livin' in Prosper today
had Miss Gretchen for English
and Miss Gail for math.
Gordon stayed on in college
but after Pearl Harbor he joined the army.
He flew missions in the Pacific until one day his
plane didn't come back.
After they heard he was missing
Miss Gretchen and Miss Gail

wore black for two years.
But then the cloud lifted and
they went back to the simple
matching dresses that they
hand-made for each other.

For more than sixty years
they taught school and
grew a summer garden.
Folks seldom saw them out
except on Sundays or at the Fourth of July
or Memorial Day Ceremony.
They never missed a Memorial Day Ceremony.
They were honoring their brother Gordon.
Except when they were in the classroom
they were always together
like a double vision or a pair of slender reeds
clad in cheap cotton dresses.

At the start of school
sometime in the early 90's
Miss Gretchen and Miss Gail
introduced their classes to a parrot
an African Grey Parrot.
His name was Archimedes because
when he first saw the double vision of them
coming into the big city pet store
he cried *Eureka!*
But the sisters introduced him to

their students as Archie.
Archie spent one day perched
in Miss Gretchen's class
and the next day perched in Miss Gail's
but every day, over the P.A., loud and clear
Archie led the whole school
in the Pledge of Allegiance.
The prompt to get him started
was to show him an American flag.
Archie took it from there.
It was an instant and continuous hit.
Soon Archie was leadin' the Pledge
at the Fourth of July and Memorial Day
Ceremonies and he was often
the guest speaker for that purpose
at the VFW and the courthouse.
Once at a Memorial Day Ceremony
down at the Courthouse
Archie was sittin' on an open perch
and a low flyover of jets startled him.
He flew into some trees near the square
too scared to come down
but when Miss Gretchen unfurled the flag
he led the Pledge from the safety of the trees.
Afterwards the Prosper Volunteer Fire
Department rescued Archie and returned him
shakin' his head
to Miss Gretchen and Miss Gail.
For almost fifteen years

Archie led the Pledge of Allegiance
every day at school and most times at
important civic affairs.

And then a few years ago Miss Gretchen
mistakenly distributed the banned book list
so carefully prepared by the school board
to her students as required reading
and Miss Gail started havin' trouble
remembering the multiplication tables
and after sixty-four years of teachin'
and moldin' the kids of Prosper
the Gardner twins retired.
Gone from the schools
but not gone from the fabric of Prosper.
Every Sunday since they arrived in 1929
Miss Gretchen and Miss Gail showed up at
the Bethel Prayer Church
(now known as the House of Prayer).
Even in their college years they came back to
Prosper religiously every Sunday.
Perfect attendance for eighty years
had to be close to a record.

And then one Sunday they didn't show up.
People looked at the empty spaces
in the pews where they always sat.
Pastor Bob looked at the empty spaces.
This was the new pastor that Miss Gretchen

and Miss Gail had still not cottoned to.
It was the new pastor who wanted
Intelligent Design taught in the schools as
an alternate theory to Evolution.
There had been a school board meeting
set to discuss it.
Lotsa folks were worried since a majority
of the school board was members
of the House of Prayer and some figgered
the skids had been greased for the measure to
pass — but **all** of the board members
had been students of Miss Gretchen
and when Miss Gretchen showed up
at the meeting and said
*If you give the idea that there are two schools of
thought concerning established science*
*— like one that says that the earth is round
and one that says the earth is flat —*
you are misleading children.
Evolution is as indisputable as the earth is round.
*Intelligent design should be considered
an alternative only in Sunday school.*
That's where it belongs, if anywhere.
Pastor Bob never even got up and spoke.

After the service with the two empty pews
no one talked about the sermon.
No one remembered the sermon.
Heck, no one heard the sermon.

The halls and the porches and the Sunday
School classes buzzed with one topic —
Where was Miss Gretchen and Miss Gail?
A delegation from the church came back from
their house with an answer everyone expected
and nobody wanted.
Miss Gretchen and Miss Gail had passed
peacefully and had gone to be with
their long-lost brother Gordon.

Everyone in Prosper went to the funerals.
The town boarded up and shut down.
People who had grown up in Prosper
but left, came back.
Beloved Rest Cemetery was overrun
with the crowd.

It wasn't much of a surprise that
Miss Gretchen and Miss Gail
left everything they had
which wasn't much
to the House of Prayer.
What most folks didn't realize was that
Pastor Bob got Archie.
Now Pastor Bob realized as well as anybody
that there was a certain amount of tension
in the air at the church ever since
Miss Gretchen challenged him on
Intelligent Design.

So when he took in Archie he devised a plan
in a sneaky, secret Pastor Bob kinda way.
He thought of it as a subtle revenge.
He decided he would remake Archie
by teaching him to recite
the Twenty-third Psalm.
He coached and he coached and he coached.
Finally Archie had it down cold.
Time after time he could say it perfectly
word for word.

Pastor Bob promoted the Sunday
when he was gonna introduce the new Archie
with all of his evangelical fervor.
He told everyone in town that the service
was gonna have a special guest
and everyone would have a special
opportunity to hear the Word
in a way they had never heard it before.
When the anointed Sunday arrived
the House of Prayer was packed.
As we sat down, folks was surprised to see
Archie perched beside the pulpit.
Everyone knew Archie
but no one had come to church that Sunday
expectin' to say the Pledge of Allegiance.
Pastor Bob breezed through
the first part of the service.
then he said *And from the mouth of God's creature*

and with a sweep of his arm like he was
introducin' the rodeo queen
he turned to Archie.

Archie knew his new cue and started
perfectly: *The Lord is my Shepherd* he said
but when he got to *He restoreth my soul*
Archie paused and said loudly and clearly
Hot Damn that's good whiskey!
Pastor Bob looked like he had swallowed
a jar of clabbered milk.
He hurriedly removed Archie from the
sanctuary and before they got to the pastor's
study everyone heard Archie repeat
clear as a bell *Hot Damn that's good whiskey!*
With Archie safely behind the hastily closed
door of his study Pastor Bob came back
and finished the service but the elders
visited him that evening, and in a month
he had resigned and moved from Prosper.

Archie was rescued from Pastor Bob by
the Wednesday Night Bible Study Class
of the House of Prayer.
He resumed leading the Pledge of Allegiance
at school and at civic events, perfectly and
without a hitch until three years ago
on the anniversary of the Gardner twins'
passing Archie fell silent from his perch.

And PK (as PK usually does) came up with a
slick solution for the issue of buryin' Archie
in Beloved Rest Cemetery.
He opened an adjacent pet cemetery called
Resting Too and buried Archie in a prime plot
complete with a ceremony that included
the Pledge of Allegiance.
The plot in Beloved Rest between
Miss Gretchen and Miss Gail
was dedicated to Gordon with twenty-one
guns and a flyover and the Gardner triplets
were together again in spirit.

Resting Too has been quite popular in Prosper.
Lots of dogs, cats, even a goat and a horse
have found their peace there
but so far only one African Grey Parrot.
And the story that PK told
that cracked us up this morning
is about a little boy who, walkin' through
the pet cemetery with his parents
strugglin' to read the headstones
tracin' the letters with his fingers, said
Look what's buried here:
Archie, a frickin' Grey Parrot.

Chauncey Cooter

Me and PK was on a field trip.
We was goin' over to Chauncey Cooter's
Flagpole Ranch to see that tiny bird
that was causing such a fuss.

We followed Chauncey's main dirt road
just like he said
and as we got closer to NeverDry Creek
we saw the patch of trees south of the road
just like he said.
We drove until we saw several cars parked
and a card table sittin' next to the fence
right beside a set of climb-over steps
just like he said.

Chauncey said he had to put that climb-over
in because so many greenhorn city folks
was gettin' stuck in the bobbed wire
or was tearin' it up tryin' to get through.

There on the table was a Big Chief tablet.
On the front was this note:

> *Please sign the book and note*
> *the time you come and the time you go.*
> *Bird has been hanging around the springs*
> *in the grove of trees just south of here.*

Watch for rattlesnakes!
Don't spook the cattle!
Carry out your trash!

Chauncey

I reckon a Rare Bird Alert travels faster
than a prairie grass fire
'cause the book was brimmin' with names.
When we signed in we saw signatures from
Maine to California, Florida to Oregon
even Australia, India and England.
All of this in about two weeks
once Chauncey agreed for them fellas from the
University to let it out they had seen
this small brown bird that was so lost.

While I was looking at the book decypherin'
some scratchy handwriting a lady came
walkin' across the pasture from the trees.
Seen it she said as she signed out
now I gotta get back home.
When she was gone I noted from the list
that she was from New Jersey
and she had been here about half an hour.

Well lookee here I says to PK
as he was inspectin' the book
Here comes Chauncey hisownself.

As we looked down the fence line
we could see a man on horseback
steadily approaching.
When he saw my pickup
and recognized me and PK
he waved and howdied
and got down off his horse.

You've seen riders like Chauncey.
Sits in the saddle like it was a lounge chair
wearin' blue jeans, chaps, boots
a ten gallon hat and with an impressive
beer belly and no assotol.
You had to wonder when was the last time
he saw his belt buckle
which was facin' straight down to the ground
and how his pants stayed up.

Now Prosper has plenty of cowboys
and some might call Chauncey a cowboy
but Chauncey was a horseman.
He had made a pretty good life training horses
and had spent more quality time
with horses than with humans.
He knew horses better than humans
and liked horses better than humans.
Chauncey was beyond a horse-whisperer.
He had regular ongoing and meaningful
conversations with them.

One time, to settle up a trainin' fee
Chauncey took a quarter horse exercise pony
that one of his training clients
was about to ship out to a farm.
The skinny awkward quarter horse
was named Flagpole.
Chauncey grew to love that little horse
with its splayed legs and big heart.
It was the first racehorse he ever owned.
In his spare time he trained Flagpole for racin'
and even entered him in a few races.
Flagpole never won, but in each race
he got stronger and finished closer.
Chauncey eventually agonized over whether
he could afford the entry fee
for a high-dollar race coming up.
He knew about all the high-powered
high-dollar horses entered in the race.
Then one day, after a hard early morning
workout Chauncey swears Flagpole
said to him *Come on let's do this.*
Chauncey pawned his car
emptied his mattress
ponied up the entry fee
and the little horse dusted the field
and created Chauncey's nest egg
which he and Flagpole parleyed into
Chauncey's comin' back to Prosper

buyin' this ranch and runnin' a world-famous
horse training facility.

Chauncey can sure enough train horses
race horses, cuttin' horses, jumpin' horses
polo horses or just ridin' horses.
He could teach a horse to play the banjo
in a bluegrass band if he took a mind to it.
Does it mostly by talkin' to them.
When I ast, he told me the same thing that
Miss Gail used to say trying to teach me math
all those years ago — *I can explain it to you
but I can't understand it for you.*

Chauncey, like PK, was one of the few
who left Prosper and came back.
His comin' back was mostly because ranches
were cheaper here than in California
or even New Mexico where he made his stash.
But his leavin' Prosper many years ago was
not exactly routine and had some in Prosper
sorta torn up. He might coulda stayed
but it was getting' complicated so he left.
Some folks were downright angry
the way it came down.

Back in high school, Chauncey was best friend
and runnin' buddy with Billy Jack Clements.

Some say Billy Jack
was dumb as a sack of hammers.
He once told Miss Gretchen
that the opposite of irony was wrinkly.
But Chauncey was his pal and good friends
don't let you do stupid things alone
so the two of them was havin' fun
constantly stirrin' things up
mostly harmless stuff like the time they
sawed a car in half and welded it back
together around the school flagpole.
Another time they rearranged the letters on
Prosper High School to read:

cool PigS Hope

Most folks thought it was purdy funny.
The principal didn't — called them vandals
which led to the prank that created the most
stir when Chauncey and Billy Jack
sorta borrowed the principal's horse overnight
and put him in the second floor school library.
Since it's way harder to get a horse to go
down stairs than it is to get him to go up
school had to be suspended
while they figured out how to get him down.
Finally Chauncey volunteered
and was able to talk him down.
Principal didn't appreciate the humor

in that particular prank.
He filed a complaint on Chauncey and
Billy Jack for stealing his horse.

Now horse thievery is considered
a very serious offense in this state.
The principal and the D.A.
both of whom had wearied of
how to deal with those two pranksters
agreed to drop charges
and to let them graduate
if Chauncey and Billy Jack would
leave Prosper and join the military.
Chauncey saw it as a good time
and a good way to get out of Prosper
so he and Billy Jack signed up for
the Marine Corps — Semper Fi.
Less than a year later they were in
real live combat units in Korea.
Chauncey was training a horse
name of Sergeant Reckless to carry
ammunition under enemy fire
to mountain-top gun placements.
Billy Jack ran a motor pool until one day
he and a Chinese mortar round
arrived at the same place at the same time.

After the war Chauncey wandered from ranch
to ranch in the West training horses.

In New Mexico he got into training
quarter horses for racing.
It was there that Flagpole talked him
into risking it all and they came up big.

Talking to us Chauncey was shaking
his head about the bird event going on.
Some people are plumb crazy he said
Then, changin' the subject he said
*I ain't got but a mile of fence left to ride.
After you guys see Tweety Bird
come on down for a drink.*

PK and me sidled on over to the grove of trees.
We found the spring but we didn't rightly
know exactly what we was lookin' for.
We saw a few different birds.
We didn't know their names
but I reckon they didn't know ours either.

Clouds were movin' in
and the sky looked awful black and furious.
I says to PK *The weather ain't hit yet
but it looks like it's just about fixin' to.
Let's go on over to Chauncey's.*
When we got within a quarter of a mile
of the ranch house we could see Old Glory
flying over the Marine Corps flag
and when we drove into the yard we could see

that the flag pole came right up out of the middle of a 1949 Cadillac.
We figgered we was at the right place.

Changin' Your Plaque

Several months ago me and PK was
just warmin' up a discussion about
whether there was exceptions
to Aristotle's Law of Non-Contradiction
when Jake and Jenny Golightly
come in to fill their thermoses
with Mary's high octane coffee.
Their rig was parked outside
with the diesel runnin' so we knew
they must be fixin' to move something
from somewhere to somewhere else.

Before they opened
the Gas & Junk Food Emporium
Jake and Jenny had about the most
interesting job in Prosper or
more accurately based out of Prosper.

Jake and Jenny made a right good living
haulin' animals from where they was
to where they needed to be
and not just cows to and from the feed yards.
At first it was trophy deer from
breeding farms to high-fenced ranches
where they was pastured
and then for big bucks
the big bucks was shot.

Jake learned to cut up garden hoses
into ten inch sections and put them
on each tine of each antler of each deer
to keep them from gettin'
chipped or broke in transit.
And sometimes the deer would be released
before Jake and Jenny retrieved all of their
hose-sleeves and trophy bucks with bright
green tines could be seen all over the ranches
until they knocked the hoses off
or got knocked off theirveryownselves.

Over the years their hauling business
evolved and grew and thrived
'cause they were so careful and trustworthy
and 'cause they had a custom trailer
with changeable cage compartments.
Soon they were transportin' tigers
and cobras and bears and mountain gorillas
from zoo to zoo or gaggles of ostriches
from isolated ranches all over the Southwest
to an ostrich slaughter house
in central Arizona or just about any
abused, emaciated or confiscated animal
from the SPCA to some remote rehab farm.
They got calls from zookeepers, ranchers
sheriffs and rich folks who had just grown
tired of the tigers they had roaming out back.
Jake and Jenny would relocate most anything.

One time a seven hundred pound grizzly bear
came out of his tranquilizer-induced stupor
before they got to the zoo where it was goin'.
Jake could tell from the weight shifts
in the trailer that the bear
had somehow got out of his cage
leavin' the only thing between him
and one of America's biggest cities
to be the metal door at the end of the trailer.
And there was the time the rig jackknifed
on an icy highway and thirteen ostriches
found themselves traipsin' around rural
Nebraska in snow up to their drumsticks.
And Jenny remembered the time that PETA
called them to assist a chicken farm in
Alabama whose unit housing fifty thousand
young chickens bound for the table
had been destroyed by a tornado.
Feathers, chickens and chicken parts were
everywhere — in trees, in fields, in bushes.
Whatever living pieces they could find
they gathered and delivered to PETA
who took in the injured survivors
that were just days away from becoming
Chick-fil-A or Colonel Sanders
and paid a team of veterinarians
to repair broken wings
splint broken legs
reattach various chicken strips

and bind up all manner of wounds.
Jake and Jenny drove away from that one
shakin' their heads.

So I ast that day *How come you guys
are back on the road?*
Well says Jenny *a friend of ours, the sheriff
of a town outside Gary, Indiana called in a bind.
Seems he and his deputies raided a place that
was a combination meth lab and chinchilla farm.
Now in shuttin' down the meth lab
they had pretty much shut down the chinchilla farm
and the sheriff had no desire or capacity
to care for the chinchillas so he declared them
forfeited under Indiana's civil forfeiture law
and sold them to a fellow in North Carolina.
So you need us to haul chinchillas from Indiana
to North Carolina?* Jenny ast the sheriff.
Not exactly said the sheriff
*Seems like the guy in North Carolina
after he paid for the chinchillas
turned up strangled with a steel banjo string.
So do you guys know someone who
will take eighty chinchillas?*

Jenny called a rehab farm near San Antonio
that had always been the place of last resort
when they was actively haulin'.
It had taken in three mangy tigers

and an elephant with an ingrown toenail
from a circus that was goin' out of business.
Those animals needed plenty of space
and were expensive to feed and house
but the old coot who ran the place
had a heart bigger than his brain
and he couldn't say no to any animal in need.
So Jenny called him and asked him
if he could take eighty chinchillas.
She asked about the elephant and the tigers.
Elephant died last year
and the tigers are long gone.
Not much here anymore.
I've kinda lost my passion for it.
Frankly since my partner and I had that fight
I ain't near so much into it.
I reckon my give-a-shitter is broke.
But if you can get them here
I can always use eighty chinchillas.

Well they hauled those rascals and left them
but Jenny didn't have a good feeling.
The place which had always been
neat and clean was getting a little run down.
The only animals they saw were
a toothless old lion lying in the sun and
a lone penguin who looked sadly out of place.
A month or so later Jenny called
to check up on the old man.

Never got no answer.
Several more tries got the same result.
So she called the local sheriff.
It appears the old man killed the chinchillas
sold the pelts and ground their little nekkid
bodies up and fed them to the lion.
The lion was still there, still lyin' in the sun,
but no trace of the old man or the penguin.

Jake showed up at Forty-Two the other night
looking lower than a worm's ankles.
He and Jenny had their rig for sale.
Following the shutdown
of the San Antonio Rehab Center
and on account of how it shut down
and with the increased cost of diesel fuel
they just decided that the chinchillas
were their last load and they were gettin' out
of the specialty animal haulin' business.
Me and Jenny is Changin' Our Plaque he said.
From now on we're simply proprietors
of Jake's Gas & Junk Food Emporium.

Now in Prosper "Changin' Your Plaque"
has a special meaning.
"Changin' Your Plaque" in Prosper
means takin' a new and better approach
to a painful situation — facin' reality
and lettin' everyone know

you're dealin' with it.
And it has that meaning
because of Jake.

Seems that growin' up in Prosper
Jake had a very special status.
It went like this:
In 1920 Jake's granddaddy J.W. Golightly
was a kid in Brooklyn New York.
He and his father J.R. Golightly
attended a baseball game in which
J.W. scrambled for and retrieved
a baseball hit by Babe Ruth.
The baseball became a family heirloom.
When Jake was playin' Little League
and later high school baseball
his dad J.J. would let Jake bring the ball
to the baseball banquet for all to see.
Right there on the horsehide
in ink that was faint and fading
was **Babe Ruth 1920.**

Even though the ball belonged
to Jake's grandfather everyone
including Jake
assumed it would eventually be Jake's
and that was reinforced by the fact that when
Jake opened his Gas & Junk Food Emporium
J.W. let Jake display it in

a special-made bullet-proof case.
In the case was the ball.
On the case was this plaque:

On loan from J.W. Golightly. Caught by him in September 1920 in New York City. It was Babe Ruth's fiftieth home run of the year. He would finish the year with more home runs than fourteen of the fifteen major league teams.

That ball became quite an attraction.
People drove from all over to see it
and bought lots of gas and junk food.

Then the unspeakable happened.
At age 92 J.W. got throwed from his horse
punctured a lung and
died in the hospital of pneumonia.
Before he died, he called Jake in.
The ball is yours he said
but there is more to the story.
It wasn't a home run — it was a foul ball.
I didn't catch it — a nice fella did and gave it to me.
It wasn't hit by Babe Ruth — I wrote that on there because he was my hero.
It wasn't even a Yankees game — it was the Giants.
But it is a baseball from 1920 — and it's yours.

Down at the Gas & Junk Food Emporium
for weeks after his grandfather's death
Jake teared up every time he looked at the ball
and especially every time he read the plaque
but when the hurting eased a bit
he knew what he had to do.
He changed the plaque.
Now, even though the **Babe Ruth 1920**
is still barely visible, the plaque simply reads:

BASEBALL RETRIEVED BY J.W. GOLIGHTLY IN NEW YORK CITY, SEPTEMBER 1920.

So if you and Jenny are Changin' Your Plaque
and givin' up the haulin' I ast
How come you're still so down?

Sometimes late at night said Jake
I think about that penguin
and wonder where he is and how he's doin'.

EDEN

Me and PK was finishin'
our first cup of Mary's coffee
discussin' last week's epic match
and the glory it brought to Prosper
and what kind of retaliation to expect
when Mary comes up with a refill
and two pieces of wild plum pie.

My treat she says *but it's just for the regulars
When this is gone, it's gone.
I ain't picking any more plums this year.
When I was reaching over the fence
to pick some really good ones
I looked down and my boot
was right beside a rattlesnake.
Absolutely scared me half to death.*

It truly was a treat to have a slice
of Mary's wild plum pie.
Sometimes when she got wild plums
she made plum ketchup.
Sometimes she made plum wine.
But when she made pies
she made the best pies in the county.

I knew PK wanted to lick the plate
as he finished his pie but our attention
went back to last week's match

and he ast me how this feud got started
this feud between Prosper and Eden.

The pioneers who first hunkered down in the
edge of these high plains were optimistic.
Hence the names of the first two settlements:
Prosper and Eden.
As they moved farther west
their more practical side came out.
Towns were named Shallowater, Levelland,
Plainview, Brownfield, Needmore, Earth.
You could include Boring
but truth be known that outpost
was named for a frontier scout
named Ezra P. Boring.

Prosper and Eden have been rivals
from the beginning.
Each of them wanted to be
county seat of Shoemaker County.
Neither got it. The choice was Boring.
Most folks from Prosper today
think of Eden as its evil stepsister.
Eden clearly has a darker side.

Prosper has 'Tipper's, a clean quiet bar
a good place for a cowboy or a farmer
to take his girl after boot-scooting or bowling.
Eden has Booger's, a dimly-lit smoky saloon

where they check you at the door for firearms
so they can issue you one if you forgot yours.

Prosper got the co-op gin
and the county fairgrounds.
Eden got the county jail
and associated bail bondsmen.
The county courthouse is
thirty miles from each in Boring.
Prosper got the John Deere dealership.
Eden got Kubota.

One year, Eden High had
an amazing basketball player.
He was All-State and went on to play in
the Final Four with Duke.
He only missed four free throws
all year his senior year of high school
but against Prosper he missed three
at the end of the game
to lose the game for their only loss.
He and his family was run out of town.

Football and basketball teams
don't play each other anymore.
Too dangerous.
Too many guns in the stands.
One year Prosper and Eden
were set to meet in the football playoffs.

Had to flip a coin to see who moved on.
Prosper's maybe best team ever was sidelined
by a coin toss — shoulda called heads.

Eden posted a new sign at the city limits:
Come and Live in Paradise:
Walk in the Garden.
Prosper followed with its own:
Live Long in Prosper.
Prosper held a 10K run with a highly
publicized cowboy boot division.
Next year Eden added a flip-flop
division to theirs.

Sometimes the rivalry escalated.
Mary had won the pie-making ribbon
at the county fair for six straight years.
A group from Eden got her disqualified
from competin' after she opened
Mary's Free Will Café
'cause she was a "professional."

So when Eden decided to create
a tourist attraction by building
an elaborate garden on the edge of town
planting, watering and feeding fig trees
and all kinds of plants that don't
naturally grow on the high plains
and when they promoted a

Grand Opening of The Garden
several cowboys from Prosper
went over the night before and released
about a hundred rat snakes, bull snakes
and garter snakes in The Garden
"Just to help with the authenticity."

But the latest installment of this saga
unfolded only last week.
For a coupla years Eden has had a sign
on the highway that says:
**Eden, Home of This Year's State Champion
Tennis Player, Dora Bunch.**
People who knew Dora thought it was a joke.
But it was not an alternate reality.
It was pure true absolute fact.

Dora had been an ordinary casual tennis
player until she turned eighty-five.
On a whim she entered
the state tennis tournament
eighty-five and older division.
She lost her match that year
to a player from Houston.
It was the only match in the division.

The next year Dora entered again but her rival
had died and Dora was crowned champion
without playing a match.

Dora entered and won by default
five straight years.
It looked like she could win from a wheelchair
or even her deathbed
especially since she had moved up
to the ninety and over bracket.
But Prosper's own Mildred "Millie" Hunt
decided it should be otherwise.
Millie was actually Dora's second cousin
by marriage and some suspected it was more
than civic pride that stirred her.

Millie was also a year older than Dora
but she was tougher than a wrangler's boot
and came to this not from a nursing home
but straight from a working ranch.
No one much in Prosper played tennis
but Millie had played a little in college
only about seventy years ago so
she figured she could go
two or three sets if needed.

The match was to be held in Abilene
because the state meet moved
from year to year.
No one knew who would show up.
Odds were pretty good that if either
was actually present at the start time
she would be declared the winner.

But never underestimate the will
of a champion or a ninety-year-old woman.

At the appointed time
at the appointed court
Dora and Millie both arrived
with their respective posses.
After a warm-up session
cut short to conserve energy
the match was on.
One hundred and eighty-three years
of experience on that court.
Dora had to serve underhanded
because her shoulder wouldn't allow her
to get the racket over her head.
Millie with her bowlegged stride
was able to retrieve some pretty wide shots
and noticing Dora's limitations
she began to lob the ball
so it bounced above Dora's head.
At the fourth court change
as the players sat and toweled off
Dora threw in her towel
and the match was over.

After their roadies gathered
and packed the gear, the competitors
hugged and walked off together
talking about grandkids, great-grandkids

and even great-greats.

But the trophy came to Prosper
and the sign came down at Eden
and Millie insisted no sign for her.
She and Dora had a pact
not to enter any more
to rest on their respective laurels
and leave tennis to the eighty-five year olds.

I looked around and might near
everybody had a piece of pie.
I reckon Mary has got a lot
of morning regulars.
And I thought back on what she said
that there would be no more plum pies
and my mind skipped ahead to ruminate
on the rest of what she said and I ast PK
What would happen
if you were scared half to death — twice?

The next day when Mary opened up
there was two bushels of wild plums
sittin' at the front door.

Ruby Foster

Coffee time at Mary's
and PK had hardly touched his coffee.
Folks were slumped in their booths
talking in whispers
and when Mary came to refill PK's cup
he just shook his head and waved her away.
Without a word she went on to the next booth.

PK said he wasn't going to Beloved Rest today.
He'd be there tomorrow
greeting folks with words of comfort and hope
but not today. Tomorrow's funeral
would be bigger than the Gardner twins'.
It would stretch the capacity of Beloved Rest
Funeral Home and Cemetery.
Everyone in Shoemaker County would be there
young, old, rich, poor, cowboys, drifters.
Everyone. Even Joe Bob Frasher
close to finishing his sentence
was able to get special parole
to attend the funeral of Ruby Foster.

Mary's eyes were puffy and red.
I loved that angel Ruby she said.
Ruby owns this building
that we call Mary's Free Will Café.
Wouldn't take any rent back when
Mary's ex Ted left with that gypsy gal

and Mary was struggling to get by.
PK stared at his coffee
steam condensing up under his eyes
'cause he had been a witness to the will and
he knew that Ruby left the building to Mary.

Most everybody had a favorite story about Ruby
— some funny, some profound.
Like the time when MayBob Holley
showed up to Bingo wearing her yoga teeshirt
that said **"Be in the Now"** and
Ruby cracked up and cleaned his glasses
thinking it said **"Pee in the sNow."**

When the wildfire took the Garza's house
at the edge of town it was Ruby
who put together a community build-out.
Then Ruby measured and sawed and nailed
right along with the Garzas
'til they were able to move on in.

There was the time that Ruby was visiting
Mrs. Hunt at the Happy Trails Living Center
and had to break up a fight between
two old biddies over which soap opera
they would watch on TV. The next week Ruby
brought a recorder so they could watch
them both and then negotiated
a schedule of who went first.

'Bout a month later no one could remember
how to program the recorder
but that was OK because one of the blue hairs
had changed her nap schedule and there was
no longer a conflict to be resolved.
In another month no one even remembered
the cause of the disagreement
but Ruby's recorder was important
to the staff because they knew that
problems that go away by themselves
come back by themselves.

When the pipes burst at the high school
it was Ruby who told the school board
which was faced with a terrible decision
*You pay for the band, the orchestra and the field trips
and I'll take care of the plumbing repairs.*
— a promise that eventually turned into
an entire new gymnasium because Ruby knew
that once those programs were unfunded
they might go away forever.

Although Ruby never had any
Ruby loved children. For forty years Ruby
gave every new mother in Prosper
rich or poor a baby blanket and a book
in English or Spanish to read to their new baby
and Ruby saw that the library
was always well-stocked with books and

adequately stocked with computers
even though Ruby frowned on screen time.
Ruby sponsored a reading club
a drama club and a chess club in Prosper.

And Ruby vigorously supported
youth outdoor activities too
sports, including baseball, rodeo
and cutting horse competitions.
Two degrees of separation connected
Ruby Foster to everything in Prosper.
Ruby had a house in the country
but lived in the heart of Prosper.

PK fought through the next day
as Prosper said goodbye to Ruby.
He checked off the list of details
that Ruby had left
placing a thermos of Mary's coffee
carefully inside as the coffin was closed.

He made it through the memorial.
He had been to dozens.
He made it through the graveside service.
He made it as people reluctantly filed away.
He made it until a week later when
without the whole town around
it came time to set the stone.

It was a simple stone.
At the top was carved a coffee cup.
It was uncomplicated like Ruby.

The marker simply read:

Matthew Reuben

Foster

1930-2017

Friend

Next morning PK went to visit the site
to make sure everything was perfect.
Sitting on top of the stone was a coffee mug
a mug he had seen many times before
imprinted with the familiar words:

> Mary's Free Will Café
> First Cup of the Day

It was full of the hottest blackest coffee
this side of the nearest branding fire.

PK wept.

Author Bio

The path that Robert E. "Bob" Wood took to *The Prosper Chronicles* was a circuitous one. Raised on the High Plains of Texas, he spent his summers working in the gas fields, farms and ranches of West Texas. These experiences convinced him to complete his education. After graduating from Texas Tech University undergraduate and Vanderbilt Law School, he spent almost thirty years practicing corporate and banking law with thirteen years teaching at Texas Tech Law School and the University of South Carolina sandwiched in the middle. Always a closet poet, he turned more attention to poetry after retirement. His poems have appeared in both printed and electronic reviews and in the *Great American Wise Ass Poetry Anthology*. In penance for writing The Prosper Chronicles, Bob is a fan of the Texas Rangers Baseball team and Texas Tech Football.

MEZCALITA PRESS

An independent publishing company dedicated to bringing the printed poetry, fiction, and non-fiction of musicians who want to add to the power and reach of their important voices.

CPSIA information can be obtained
at www.ICGtesting.com
Printed in the USA
FFHW02n0144091018
48735844-52816FF